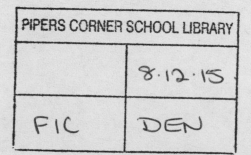

Too Cool
for
School

Also by Grace Dent

DIARY OF A CHAV
Trainers V. Tiaras
Slinging the Bling
Ibiza Nights
Fame and Fortune
Keeping it Real

DIARY OF A SNOB
Poor Little Rich Girl
Money Can't Buy Me Love

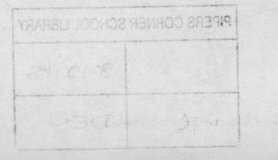

Too Cool for School

Grace Dent

Hodder
Children's
Books

A division of Hachette Children's Books

For Mam and Dad

This diary belongs to:

Shiraz Bailey Wood

Address: 10a Paramount Mansions,
             Paramount Road,
             Whitechapel,
             London,
             E1 7RQ

AUGUST

SATURDAY 1ST AUGUST

10pm in my room – Goodmayes, Essex.

THINGS SHIRAZ BAILEY WOOD WON'T MISS ABOUT 34, THUNDERSLEY ROAD WHEN SHE BEGINS HER SLAMMING SUPERFLY NEW LIFE IN LONDON WITH CARRIE DRAPER . . .

* Mrs Diane Wood, my mother, quizzing me 'bout where I'm going, for how long and who with EVERY SINGLE TIME I put on my pink hoodie and hoops.

* Miss Cava-Sue Wood, my pregnant sister, quacking on about her 'tingly nipples' and her weak 'pelvic floor' and making us watch screaming women with their knees by their ears on the Baby Channel when I'm trying to eat my Bombay Badboy pot noodle.

* Penny, our morbidly obese Staffy, waking me up for her breakfast at 6am on Sunday mornings by squeaking her squeaky Bart Simpson doll. Then trying to eat my toe-jam.

* Murphy Wood, my little brother, in the room next door to mine, shaking his bed proper quick for four minutes every night before he falls asleep. What is he doing???

* The sound each day at approximately 8.10 am after my father, Mr Brian Wood has visited the lav, when he shouts 'Woo-hoo! No-body light a match!'

* Wesley Barrington Bains II, my ex-boyfriend texting 'the luv hour' on Essex FM five times a week dedicating the song 'Lonely'by Akon' to 'his little shorty shizzlebizzle who he's gonna miss so much, innit.'

Wesley, bruv, we iz OVER, YOU GET ME?

* I won't miss my Aunty Glo coming 'round our house every Saturday night with a ropey movie she's bought off those Vietnamese geezers in ASDA car-park and her bloody karaoke machine. There will be NO karaoke Westlife in London.

* Most of all I won't miss the fact that nearly all these clowns mentioned above have the flipping BRASS NECK to treat me like I'm still a kid when I, SHIRAZ BAILEY WOOD am seventeen years old! I'm practically a bloody woman. Deal wiv-it!!!

Well, asta la vista Wood family! Ha ha LMAO! I'm moving to London with Carrie Draper! Laterz Goodmayes! Goodbye Superchav Academy! London babeeeeey. Yeeeeeah!

4 am – My bedroom – still awake.

Oh my days. I totally can't SLEEP. I mean, it's not like I'm bricking it about moving to London or nothing. No way. I'm Shiraz Bailey Wood – I'm nails me. It's just I've been thinking about stuff I might miss if I leave home . . .

STUFF SHIRAZ BAILEY WOOD WILL POSSIBLY MISS ABOUT 34, THUNDERSLEY ROAD WHEN SHE BEGINS HER SLAMMING NEW LIFE IN LONDON WITH CARRIE DRAPER:

1. I'll miss when Nan and her husband Clement come over on a Sunday and Nan roasts a chicken and some spuds and she makes all the outside of the spuds proper crispy and they soak up the gravy well nice and she even roasts a few extra ones and leaves them on a saucer for me in the fridge to microwave on Monday.
(NOTE: Must find out what food is on offer in London. Will I have to live on those toasted ham punani things from Starbucks? Christ on a sledge – I hope not. I had one of them on a Geography trip once. It tasted like old badger muff).

2. I'll miss it when me and Cava-Sue go to Spirit of Siam Chinese together to fetch the family's set meal D and we always buy a SECRET EXTRA SPRING ROLL out of Mum's money to eat on the way back and we laugh like mad 'cos greedygob Murphy ain't getting any of it. It is the BESTEST tasting spring roll ever.

3. I'll miss the times when I paint Mum's toenails for her before she goes somewhere special like Goodmayes Social, 'cos it's not like we get on that well usually, but just for those five minutes we're like bezzies and Mum always fiddles about with my hair and I always call her feet 'hooves' and she laughs her head off. Then afterwards mum dances up the stairs with bits of tissue between her toes singing 'I'm Too Sexy For My Feet' and I wolf whistle her. I'll miss that.

4. I'll miss when me and our Murph watch EastEnders and we pretend that we know the plot already. Like Murph says, ''Ere Shiz, I KNOW what happens tonight! The Vic gets hit by a meteor!'

'Oh really Murph?' I say, 'Well I know what happens tonight! Scientists find out that Phil Mitchell's head is made of Dairylea cheese!' Then we laugh and laugh. No one else finds it jokes. Only me and Murph.

5. I'll miss the times when it's raining on a night and I'm sitting indoors in my room reading *Heat* and our Penny

mooches in and curls up under the duvet like a hot water bottle and we end up asleep, with her head on the pillow snoring. Silly fat Pen.

6. I'll miss when my dad winks at me when I'm on my way out to Ilford Mall and slips me a fiver and says 'Don't tell yer mother, you'll get me shot!'

7. I've got a feeling that I'll *really* miss Wesley Barrington Bains II.

Yeah. I know. I know I say we've OVER. But it ain't TOTALLY over is it? I mean, we don't snog each other no more or nothing but we're still proper good mates. We have been since back in the day. I love my Wesley to bits.

I just don't love him like, y'know, THAT. Least I don't think I do. Or do I? No . . . I don't. Especially now his hair is getting a bit of a sunroof on the top where his head is poking out. Bless. But I really don't think I still love him. Do I? Oh my life. I'm proper confused.

My mother – who is a world authority on EVERYTHING – reckons first love is the deepest. My mother reckons you always care about them a little bit. My mother knows this 'cos her first love when she was sixteen was this geezer called Trevor from Chadwell Heath who she binned 'cos she fancied my dad more 'cos my dad had a Mini Cooper and liked going down

Southend while all Trevor had was eczema and a pet ferret.

So anyways, my mother reckons you never stop caring 'bout your first love. 'There's always a spark,' my mother says. Whatever that bloody means.

What if I don't meet anyone else who properly gets who I am in London? What if all I meet is snotty folk who think I'm just a chav?

But HANG ON A MINUTE, why do I bloody care if they do? I'm only keeping it real! And where will me and Carrie live? And what sort of job will I get? And And why, oh, why does Aunty Glo reckon she can sing all the hard bits of 'Living La Vida Loca' when she actually sounds like one of them Oods off of Dr Who with its wibbly things in the TARDIS door?

And why is this house so noisy!!? And why does London not seem like a very good idea no more? And why have I got the bogtrots coming on? Is it 'cos we all had our dinners out of the 'Oops! Reduced' section of Asda again? And what is my mother's OBSESSION with making the Wood family eat nearly out of date pork products that no one else in Essex wants – not even folk who pay with council tokens!!?

And why is my life always filled with far more questions than answers?

And when I move to London, will I ever get the proper bling-bling, mega life I've been dreaming about? Or will I end up like a crack-head homeless who sits by cash machines with pheggy bits round their mouths and golden crispy patches in their arm-pit region?????

Right, that's it. I'm texting Carrie first then when I wake up.

I'm bloody staying in Goodmayes.

SUNDAY 2ND AUGUST

So I meets my best mate Carrie Draper this morning by the bandstand in Goodmayes park. Carrie wants to do some 'power-walking', 'cos she's well obsessed with losing some inches before she starts at Butterz Beauty Academy in Covent Garden this September. Not like Carrie needs to lose any inches. She's well slinky she is, like a model. Actually, ever since she's had her hair dyed blonder and those hair extensions done last week she looks like one of them Vileda Supermops stood upside down with Maybelline mascara on. (Except a pretty Vileda mop of course – Carrie is proper pretty.)

Carrie reckons London is going to be like a whole new start for us, 'specially now she's given her Saf the boot. Carrie ain't confused about Saf at all. 'It was totally for the best,' said Carrie this morning. I asked her if he cried or nothing and she said she didn't know 'cos she hung up on him cos he was wasting her credits.

'Anyway, new look, new direction, new me, Shiz!!' she said. And I was trying to concentrate on what she was saying but to be honest I was finding it hard not to get distracted by her chest 'cos she'd bought some new 34D fake chicken fillet boobs down La Senza in Bluewater the day before an she put them in proper wonky.

Like, the left boob was sitting up all perky but the right one had sort of wandered off somewhere round her back. Like it had got bored and just fancied a nice lie down. Bare jokes, it was. Even Carrie laughed well loud when I pointed it out to her.

'Oh my life!! What am I like with my wonky scones?' Carrie said. Then we wandered over by the swings laughing our heads off and the park keeper, the one with the squashed strawberry nose came out to chuck us some evils as usual, but then he saw Carrie in her skin tight blue Nike bottoms and cropped hoodie which shows her belly button and he sort of stopped and looked.

Then Penny comes running up with a dead crow she's found near the bushes and me and Carrie both start screaming and old strawberry nose starts shouting 'DOGS MUST BE ON LEADS IN THE RESTRICTED AREAS!!!'

So Carrie starts creasing going, 'What bruv? Even this dog I'm carrying?' and she starts holding up Alexis her mother's chi-hua-hua which was sleeping under her armpit, snuggled in beside the escapee chicken fillet boob.

'Oh,' strawberry nose goes. 'I didn't even see you had a dog.' Fair enough, 'cos Alexis don't look much like a dog, in fact she looks more like a lucky gonk you might win from some pikeys down Thurrock Carnival.

So me and Carrie go and sit on those big ducks on springs that you can sit on and rock proper fast and I takes a big breath and I says to Carrie.

'Y'know, Cazza, I don't know if I can come with you to London, I've been thinking about it all last night and I reckon I'm making a big mistake.'

So Carrie stops rocking her duck and goes, 'Oh what are you chatting about now Shiz you MENTALOID?? Course you don't mean that!'

And I says, 'Yeah I do mean it Caz! 'Cos I been thinking 'bout stuff last night and well, folk like me don't just move away from Goodmayes do they?' But Carrie weren't having this, she was just looking at me like I was chatting a load of old crap.

So I says, ''Ere remember that Joshua Fallow lad I was seeing? Remember his mother who was well up herself? She used to ignore me all the time and call me a chav? Well it really made me feel like a proper hoodrat that did. It made me feel well paranoid. That silly cow looked down at me she like I was rubbish in her wheelie bin.'

'Oh, what's she got to do with anything?' Carrie says, proper rolling her eyes at me.

'Well what if everyone in London thinks it too?!' I says.

'Oh Shiz, shutttup you DONUT,' said Carrie, then she put Alexis down on the ground and the lazy thing starts yelping like it's never used its feet since 2003 or something.

'Shiraz!' Carrie says to me, 'EVERYBODY seems like a

chav to bloody Joshua Fallow's mother. Her head is right up her own 'arris. She reckons her poo don't smell!!! Like it plops out her bumhole in little pink pellets like strawberry bloody bonbons! Silly moo!'

And I started laughing a bit then just thinking about Mrs Fallow on the lav with her big knickers round her puffy ankles in her stupid en suite bathroom that every bedroom in Joshua's house has 'cos they can't stand each other's bumsmells.

Then Carrie picks up Alexis again 'cos she's whining and goes.

'So, let me get this straight, you ain't coming to London on our amazing adventure 'cos Mrs Fallow reckons you're a chav?'

But I didn't say nothing to that. I just went and stood on the roundabout and made it spin a bit. There was a time when that roundabout seemed well big and scary. Now it felt proper low and small and boring.

'So what you gonna do instead?' says Carrie.

'I ain't worked it out yet.' I shouts at her, 'cos I was spinning round and around.

Carrie starts to crease. 'Well I have Shiz, that's why I'm offski,' she says proper definite. 'I ain't staying in Essex and ending up here for ever like Kezia is with Latanoyatiqua. I ain't ending up preggo by some random and trapped here till I die. No way! I'm not like that.' Then Carrie put her hand over her gob and proper cringed.

'Oh God – sorry Shiz, I don't mean your Cava-Sue!' she

says. 'I don't think her Lewis is some random or nothing. I was meaning folk like Collette Brown who used to work down Cheeky's Vertical Tanning with her kid Rudi!'

'Oh my days!' I said. 'No one knows who Collette's baby-daddy is do they? Not even her! All she's got is a list of possible suspects!'

We both started laughing proper loud then.

'Actually, I thought Rudi was Earl's son?' I says.

'Yeah, so did Earl. And so did Biggy who does the door at Peppermint Palace too! Well I saw Collette pushing Rudi in a pram down Ilford Xchange last week and I tell you Shiz, that baby is a different colour to all of 'em. Looks oriental it does!'

We both giggled for a bit, before we remembered it ain't bare jokes at all.

'I'm sick of Goodmayes Shiz,' Carrie says to me. 'It's the most boring place in the world.'

'Yeah,' I says but I was feeling proper confused now.

''Ere Shiz? Remember that time last Christmas when we went to London with Sixth Form, and we went and saw *King Lear* and we went out to that club called *Forever Friends* and afterwards we jumped in the fountains at Trafalgar Square? And Nabila was sick on her hijab on the nightbus home and Sean bought those pills that turned out to be indigestion mints but we all felt buzzing off our heads anyhow and then you ended up snogging Josh Fallow and I stayed at Saf's and said I was at yours? Remember that Shiz?'

''Course I do,' I says to her. 'Cos, it was only like the most exciting night of my whole entire life.

'Well, we can have nights like that all the time if you come with me to London. Oh come on you donut. My dad's gonna cover our first month's rent. We got a whole month at least to get you a job! You know that don't you?'

'I know,' I says.

'How nang would that be?!' she says.

'Heavy nang.' I says. And then we didn't say anything for ages.

But then we both started laughing well loud.

'Cos by that point I was totally bloody going with her again.

And now I'm lying in bed writing this and I still think I'm going. I reckon I've got to, 'cos I can't end up trapped in Goodmayes like Collette, or my Cava-Sue.

MONDAY 3RD AUGUST

OH MY LIFE, I am SO bloody leaving this house and this family!!!

I can't believe I nearly changed my mind! I would have mugged myself RIGHT off if I had. My mother is doing my NUT right in. And honest to God I don't have anger issues like a load of the kids at Mayflower had, no way. Shiraz Bailey Wood is light 'n' breezy lemon squeezy most of the time, BUT oh lord above, sometimes my mother just makes me want to FLIP OUT.

So I just gets back from Carrie's house where we've been planning our move to London and I walks in the kitchen and there's my mother with Cava-Sue sitting at the table both eating Mr Kipking French Fancies and talking about Cava-Sue's belly, 'cos my sister's got her footless tights pulled down, and her bump resting on the table, looking like an emo spacehopper.

And they're both rabbitting about how when you're pregnant you sometimes don't do a proper poo for weeks, 'Cos you're 'all bunged up'. Then Cava-Sue announces she did push something out this morning but it was all 'Hard like a gobstopper'. And my mother says, 'Oh well, better out than in I reckon.'

Uuggh! So I warns them both that if they keep on talking about pooing I might cover them both with half-digested Quavers 'cos pooing is a private matter between yourself and the loo IN MY OPINION, 'cos I'm not being funny or nothing, but it IS.

So Cava-Sue tuts and goes, 'Oh Shiraz, grow up, it's only the human body.'

So I says, 'Yeah fair play Cava-Sue and there's nothing wrong with the human body but I wish you'd pull your leggings up 'cos I don't want to see your bush five times a day, thank you very much, it's making me queasy!'

So Cava-Sue goes, 'Oh Shiz, stop bloody exaggerating, you little brat. I'll tell you something! This is a marvellous thing that you're witnessing here! The majesty of motherhood in all its glory! Y'know, Shiraz, I'm bloody glad you're moving to London if you're going to bring negative vibes into this space, what with this foetus starting to be receptive to sounds and smells . . . in fact on page 47 of my book it says . . .'

But before she could waffle on any longer my mother quacks up, ''Ere hang on a minute? Where's our Shiraz going? Who's going to London?'

So Cava-Sue goes, 'Oh we've been through this mother! Shiraz is moving to London and her room is going to be the nursery! Shiraz is sharing a flat with Carrie Draper who's going to train at Butterz Beauty Academy to be a beautician!'

So my mother just giggles and tuts and rolls her eyes and says, 'Oh yeah. Cloud bloody cuckoo land as ever.'

Then she picks up the Ilford Bugle and pretends to be proper fascinated by a story about a 'Charity Wear A Wacky Hat-a-than' day at the local Lidl which she is SO NOT fascinated by at all. She is FAKING it.

Now this is well annoying.

'I'm going, I am,' I says to my mother.

'Yeah, 'course.' says my mother under her breath.

'Why won't I?' I says.

''Cos you ain't got no money!' she says.

'I've got a bit saved from Mr Yolk!' I says back at her. 'And I'm getting a job too!'

But my mum just snorts then and says, 'Oh, you've had jobs! You never stick at them! Half Job Bob – that's what we should call you! What about that job at the pakora factory? Ran away didn't you? And what about Mr Yolk? Couldn't handle that either. Then you're off back to school to be Little Miss Cleverclogs. But now you're sick of that and you're off to London to make your fortune with Carrie Draper. Ha! Well *bonne chance* to both of you!'

So I listens to all that and my blood is boiling by this point. The thing that drives me proper MENTAL about my mother – and believe me I love the woman I really do, I love the bones of her – the thing I HATE is how she can take a list of stuff that she knows about you, stick it all in a story with bits of the facts all wrong, then tell it all jumbled up in a way to suit herself without even looking in the least bit ashamed that she is A BIG BLOODY PANTS ON FIRE LIAR.

It's like she proper believes what she's saying. Like she's one hundred per cent right and you're in some sort of denial about the fact you're a proper wastecadet. How does she do that???? HOW????????

'Oh, Mother stop it,' Cava-Sue was saying proper gently. 'You're only saying that 'cos you're scared about Shiraz leaving home! Shiz don't listen to her! Stop it both of you!' but I wasn't taking no notice of that 'cos I was WELL vexed with my mother about the 'Half Job Bob' bit.

WHAT A FLAMING LIBERTY SHE IS!!!??? I worked at Mr Yolk for months I did!

I did my AS levels! I can come back and do the second bit some other time!

So I shout, 'Why can you never be supportive 'bout anything I want to do in my bloody life, you stupid woman!'

But inside I was thinking, 'Oh my gosh, it is EXACTLY the same fight as Cava-Sue and Mum used to have before Cava-Sue flipped out and left home a few years back!' It was like history had done a backwards loop – just like in *Dr Who* or something.

'Oh, I've gotta be supportive now?' laughs my mother, 'Of what exactly? You living on fantasy bloody island as usual. One minute you and Carrie are going to be singers and you're going on that *Million Dollar Talent Show*, next you're finishing with that lovely lad Wesley Barrington Baines II, then it's back on again, now it's off again and now you're going to London. You wanna get your head examined by Dr Gupta you do! You've got a slate off!'

'I ain't got a slate off mother! I just want to be happy!' I shouted.

'Well, if you think you'll be happy in London, there's the door,' she shouts back.

So I stormed upstairs proper angry, banging my bedroom door so loud that I accidentally knocked over that basket of peach pot pourri mum what mum puts outside the lav to hide smells 'cos we ain't got an en suite.

I'll show her. I'll bloody show them all.

WEDNESDAY 5TH AUGUST

Oh my days. Today has been long. I left the house to meet Carrie well early this morning 'cos we was off on a fact-finding mission for our slamming superfly new lives. To be honest, I could have done with a lie-in this morning, but our Cava-Sue was waving a tape-measure by my lughole at 8am measuring my room up for the bloody Mothercare 'Moses Basket' and stand what Nan has given her vouchers for. Cava-Sue reckons it might fit in the corner. Y'know once I've moved out my desk, trainers and stereo.

Charming?!

''Ere would you jump in my grave so fast?' I says to her.

'We're not giving you a grave Shiraz,' she says to me. 'Me and Murph have agreed that when you die we're going to have you fired out of a cannon into Goodmayes pond.'

'Bare jokes.' I says back to her then pulled the duvet over my head.

Pregnancy has brought out a WELL dark sense of humour in our Cava-Sue. And, honest to God, Cava-Sue don't need no more blackness in her life, wot with her being an emo. 'Cos y'know what emos are like. They're only happy when they're in their room crying about child poverty in San Salvador and listening to that geezer from Funeral for a Friend who always sings like someone's just given him a turbo wedgie he weren't expecting.

Anyway, now Cava-Sue's having this baby she's on this bloody mission 24/7 to save the planet on behalf of her unborn foetus, so she wants everything in our rubbish recycled EVEN THE CARDBOARD IN THE MIDDLE OF THE BOG ROLL so you can't even take a wazz in peace without her banging on the bog door asking if there's anything for her Tuesday bloody recycling collection! NO WONDER her Lewis takes all those extra shifts at Sunshine Sandwiches 'to save some money for the kid' – LMAO!!!

So, anyways next thing Cava-Sue puts her hands on her stomach and goes, 'Ooh movement!' and I sits up proper upright and says, 'What? The baby!?' and she goes, 'Ooh no, not the baby, my bowels. I've been up since 7am eating dried apricots hoping it might sort me out.'

And it was about then I decided to definitely move out of Thundersley Road hopefully into a place where people can grasp the concept of TOO MUCH INFORMATION and PERSONAL SPACE.

So I puts on my pink hoodie and my pale blue fake-Moschino jeans and my gold hoops and a bit of pink blusher and I leaves our house and just as I'm almost by the end of the road I hear a bike coming at me from behind, proper fast down the pavement. It's so fast I nearly have to jump into Bert at number 89's front garden. It's this really big kid with a ginger skinhead, 'bout 20 or something, flying past on a mountain bike.

Then he suddenly pulls a skid and turns round and looks me up and down and goes, 'Shiraz Bailey Wood!? Wa'gwan darling!?' and I looks at him and I can't quite work it out at first then I realise it's bloody Clinton Brunton-Fletcher, Uma Brunton-Fletcher's mentaloid older half-brother.

'Oh, hello Clinton,' I says, 'You home then?'

'You knows it, darling,' he says, sucking his teeth a bit then checking out my baps, which in fairness have grown about two sizes since he last saw me. 'I been in Portsmouth, y'know, er, working and that,' he says.

'Pah. Hiding from Janelle who was gonna murk ya,' I think to myself but don't say out loud.

'You back for long then?' I says, hoping for Uma's sake the answer is 'No'.

'Back for life, darlin' laughs Clinton, who I now see has had one of his teeth put in gold at the front, which makes him look like some sort of cyborg from the Planet Hoodrat. 'You wanna spread the word. Clinton is back.'

'Yeah, 'course,' I says to him.

''Ere, Shiraz, you looking for skunk?' he says. 'I can do ya a quarter for twenty five quid? Seen as you's lookin damn fine.'

'Nah, s'allright,' I says, zipping my hoodie round my scones.

'Need any pills? Three for a tenner? Miu Mius? Straight from Amsterdam. Proper lovely they are, won't mong you out or nuffin'.'

'Nah, thanks,' I says to him. 'I'm a bit skint.'

'I'll put em on tick if you want?' he says.

'Nah I'm OK,' I says. Sometimes I reckon the only way to avoid taking drugs in Essex would be to put a balaclava on backwards then sit in the downstairs airing cupboard with the door shut. Especially if bloody Clinton Brunton-Fletcher is back.

So I walk up to Goodmayes station thinking about Clinton and worrying what Thundersley Road will be like now he's back, shottin weed and jacking kids bikes same as bloody ever and the 5.0 arriving all times of the night to lift him and all manner of hoodrats turning up who's he's met in Portsmouth.

POOR UMA.

Then I meet Carrie who is standing outside the Goodmayes Station by the newspaper kiosk looking a bit like she's off to audition for *Britain's Next Top Model.*

Carrie's got her hair all up in a bun with a hairband pushing up the fringe. She's wearing a little green summer wraparound frock from H&M with flipflops, her toes are all French pedicured and she's got on big sunglasses. Pulled together all nice, she is. So we jump on the overground train to Stratford and after about half an hour of standing with my face nearly in a tall man's bum cleavage we end up standing in Liverpool Street Station which is sort of scary 'cos there's hundreds of folk everywhere and there's police walking about with maching guns and dogs, 'cos apparently there's been some sort of terrorist alert outside Accessorize.

And OK, it's been a false alarm but it makes me feel proper worried about going down on the London Underground, but Carrie is pulling me along to the turnstiles going, 'C'mon Shiz, don't be soft.' So we get on to the dirty silver escalators and go down, down, down on to the Central Line platform where if some nutter did set a rucksack bomb off no one up on the ground would hear us scream, in fact no one would even know me and Carrie were down here at all until we never came home again. And that makes me feel PROPER freaked out but Carrie just laughs at stuff like that and goes,

'Oh Shiz, when it's your time to go, it's your time to go. You can't do jack about it. I never think about dying, me! My ambition is to live forever. So far so good eh!!' 'Cos that's the thing about Carrie Draper, Carrie can block things out when she wants to, but I can't 'cos I'm always keep it real.

Anyways, I always think the tube in London is well weird. You sit in these long lines facing each other trying not to look in each others eyes and no one usually speaks and if someone does speak everyone pretends to be totally deaf or gives them arsey looks for spoiling their lovely silence when it's not even silent it's clanky and noisy.

So, me and Carrie sits down opposite some French lads who obviously didn't know about the no talking rule so were burbling away in French. I'm not sure what about. *Croque Monsieurs* probably, 'cos that's all any

Frenchies did all day in my French *Aujourd'hui!* GCSE text book at school.

Bloody obsessed with *Croque Monsieurs* they were. 'Oi Pierre!' I used to say to make Carrie laugh, 'It's a bloody toasted ham sandwich! Calm yerself down, bruv!! No wonders my Aunty Glo never stays more than five hours in bloody Calais when she takes her van over to stock up on booze!!!' But Madam Sibone used to shout '*Tiens Toi!*' which means shut your trap. She used to say it a lot, 'cos she could never handle me being real.

Anyway, so we're on the tube and I'm next to this bloke with big long dreadlocks and a shy looking Hassidic Jewish guy and a little Indian woman in a posh sari and a City-boy geezer in a smart suit who was drooling at his copy of *Nuts*. And I'm staring at everyone and thinking bout how people come from all over the world to London to start a new life. And I starts thinking it's a good thing that I'm leaving Goodmayes to see the world. 'Cos we can't all just stop for ever in the place we were born, just 'cos it feels normal can we? 'Cos normal is proper boring.

Then suddenly we were at Tottenham Court Rd station and Carrie poked my arm and said, 'Oi Shizniz we're getting off.'

So we wanders off down Oxford Street which is mobbed – totally ram-jam with tourists past Niketown and past the big Top Shop and the Big H&M and we SO wanna go in but we ain't got time today, then we wander back down into Covent Garden nearly getting squashed by a red double decker bus as we go, 'cos Carrie wanted to have a proper look at Butterz Beauty Academy. We've only ever seen it on *Living* Channel. It's a tall white building near the tube station with a gold door and a sign what says 'BUTTERZ'. Carrie and me took our photos standing outside so we can put them on our Bebos so folk like Latoya Bell and Chantalle Strong can see them and be WELL SICKENED.

Next we went to an area nearby called Holborn where Carrie heard about this agency that helps folk from Butterz Academy find flats. So Carrie walks in to chat to them but I'm proper distracted by the shop next door called 'Working Magic – Employment Agency.'

Well OK, truth to tell I'm more distracted by this well choong boy standing in the window display in Working Magic fiddling with the cards 'cos, OH MY LIFE he looks like something from The OC or something, with short dark hair and a pale blue shirt and black trousers and proper broad shoulders and blue eyes and MAN HE WAS BUFF. I feel proper tingly just remembering him and honest that don't happen when I think about my Wesley Barrington Bains II. I just feel totally blank with no fizzes in my nipples at all.

So the lad wanders back off into the office and that's when I see that he works in Working Magic! And I dunno what happens next 'cos next thing I'm in there, like bloody swimwear, asking him for a Working Magic application form!!!!! Ha ha ha!

He's called Danny. Danny has long brown eyelashes and one of them small buff bums you wanna bite. Danny has got a right funny voice 'cos he's from a place called Bolton so he sounds like he should be working in the knicker factory in *Coronation Street*. I told him that and he laughed well loud for ages.

Danny reckons that he might be able to get me a job well quick depending on what I write on the form. Danny says I should be real 'bout my skills though, and not exaggerate, 'cos some folk he meets are proper fake. That won't be a problem I says to Danny, 'cos Shiraz Bailey Wood always keeps it real and Danny smiled at me and says, 'Yeah, so it appears.'

Me and Carrie spent about the next five hours looking at flats in London and I'm not gonna lie it was WELL DEPRESSING, 'cos some of the flats looked like the haunted house at Dagenham Fair and some had sofas in them what a homeless might have overdosed on, but anyway the good news is we found one flat and though it didn't look much from the outside it wasn't too shoddy on the inside. And I'm falling asleep now so I can't explain it no more but the address is number 10a Paramount Mansions. It's in Whitechapel in East London. It's available from September 1st as it's just being repainted.

Ha! Paramount Mansions?!!! LMAO! Sounds well posh don't it?? Oh, it so ain't. The 'mansion' bit is a right old exaggeration just to make folk go and see it. Oh my days.

We are SO going to be keeping it real.

SATURDAY 8TH AUGUST

Clinton Brunton-Fletcher got lifted by the police tonight. The police arrived and took him on suspicion of robbing the Londis over on the Higgins Estate. I can't believe he lasted here four days really. He usually don't even have time to get his hoodie off and let the water soak in on his favourite dinner (Beef and Tomato Pot Rice) before the feds are there pushing him in the back of the bully-van AGAIN.

Tonight was a right old warm evening so everyone from Thundersley Road came out to watch. Clinton was making a big song and dance as usual. I dunno why he acts like such a man all the time 'cos when the Feds come to lift him he always screams like a little girl going, 'Yoooooooo're hurting me! Youooooooooo're hurting me! Ahhhhhhh my arm is twisted! Arrrgh!' It's sort of funny tho' 'cos he looks proper stupid. It was even more jokes tonight 'cos Bert at 89 came out and shouted 'Hit him harder officer! He stole my gnome!'

Anyways, in the middle of the screaming Uma comes out with her staffy Zeus and stands in her front garden by the fridge smoking an Embassy Red so I goes to say hello.

'All right Shiz!' she says, 'I thought you were well gone from this place? Why ain't you in London?'

And I laughs and says. 'I've not gone yet. Me and Carrie just found our flat this week and I'm looking for a job.'

So Uma goes, 'God, you are bare lucky to be getting out of here, Shiz.' And I felt proper guilty then 'cos Uma looked sort of thin and tired, standing there in her leggings and hoodie.

'You still going back to school in September? I says to her.

'And she looks at me and laughs and goes, 'Hell yeah. If my grades are OK. He ain't spoiling my life Shiz. I worked well hard for those AS levels.'

'Cos fair play to Uma, she did work hard.

'You coming down on Wednesday to get your grades?' says Uma.

'Yeah,' I said. 'I need to put them on my job application form.'

Uma just looked at me and looked a bit sad.

'So, this flat you got, what's it like then?' she says.

'Well, it's pretty crappy on the outside,' I says. 'But inside it's just being repainted. Two small bedrooms. Proper small living room. Kitchen. Shower. It's OK.' So Uma thinks for a bit like she was about to say something, but then Zeus starts whining for his dinner and when Zeus wants to be fed you just wanna feed him right away, 'cos he's got a look about him like he might just start eating a passing pram or something.

'Best go,' she says.

So I says, 'Oi, by the way what's your Clinton been lifted for?'

And Uma says, 'Oh . . . yeah, the Feds reckon he held

up Londis with a Tazer gun.'

We both watched as the police van drove off, with Clinton inside banging the side and shouting.

'He never did it, mind.' says Uma. 'He was with me indoors at the time. I can prove it.'

'Have you told the police that?' I says.

And Uma laughs and goes, 'Nah, I'll ring them in the morning. I fancy a night of peace 'cos I wanna watch X Factor.'

And then she flicks her Embassy butt into the garden and goes indoors laughing and I thought, God I'm gonna miss Uma, 'cos she is proper brand new.

WORKING MAGIC
APPLICATION FORM – 4C09 –
FOR TEMPORARY EMPLOYMENT

SURNAME: Wood
FIRST NAME: Shiraz Bailey
OTHER NAMES: The Shizniz, Shizzlebizzle, Little Shizza.
NATIONALITY: British
ADDRESS: 10a Paramount Mansions, Paramount Street, Whitechapel, London, E1, 7RQ
E-mail: *theshizz@wideblueyonder.co.uk*

EDUCATION:

Mayflower Academy, Goodmayes, Essex.

GCSE	**English Lang**	**A***
GCSE	**English Lit**	**A***
GCSE	**Mathematics**	**C**
GCSE	**Religious Stu.**	**A**
GCSE	**History**	**A**
GCSE	**French**	**B**
GCSE	**Geography**	**B**
GCSE	**Applied Sci**	**E**
GCSE	**Art**	**D**
AS	**English Literature**	**B**
AS	**History**	**B**
AS	**Film Studies**	**C**
AS	**Critical Thinking**	**A**

ANY OTHER RELEVANT INFORMATION ABOUT YOUR EDUCATION:

As you can see my AS levels aren't too shoddy, but I'll be straight up with you I'm giving the A2 part of my A-levels a swerve for a bit as I am well jacked off with school and the whole 'folk all up in my face telling me what to do' thing. Plus I want to get out of bloody Goodmayes soon before I end up stuck here for ever with a baby what is a totally different ethnicity to both me and the geez I have named to the Social as the babyfather, so I am coming to London to make my fortune instead.

COMPUTER SKILLS:

I have 748 friends on Bebo. I don't do Myspace much no more 'cos I'm sick of getting spammed by willie enlargement adverts, so if you message me there don't think I'm dissing you if I don't hit ya back. I am WELL good at PGA Golf on *Nintendo Wii* and once got to the Pyramid level on *Zombie Armageddon Bloodbath II* for the PS2 without using ANY of my Halo Lifelines.

I know my way around Windows 2000 a bit which ain't bad considering how totally gay our home computer is. The stupid bloody thing has had more viruses than Whips Cross hospital probably 'cos it only cost two hundred quid from PC world and that was including the bloody printer.

OFFICE EXPERIENCE

Yes, I have experience of sitting in our headmaster Mr Bamblebury's office on many occasions.

WHAT SORT OF EMPLOYMENT ARE YOU INTERESTED IN?

Television presenter. Author. Person who writes jokes for TV shows. Columnist for a newspaper where I just talk about what I did that day and what I think. Entertainer. Television extra work (in the Queen Vic in *EastEnders* or on *The Bill* as a crackhead or something like that). Or otherwise any job at all as I am totally BRASSIC PARK, blud.

NAME AN OCCASION IN THE PAST WHERE YOU HAVE BEEN PROUD OF YOUR ACHIEVEMENTS?

A couple of years ago I was responsible for the Mayflower Academy Winter Festival which was an end-of-school year Christmas thing 'cept we couldn't call it Christmas 'cos Mr Bamblebury is obsessed with not offending all the Muslims, which is totally wack cos I spoke to Nabila and Tariq and they ain't bovvered what you call December as long as they get a Cadbury's selection box and a fortnight of lie-ins. Anyways, the festival involved loads of singing and dancing and non-alcoholic mulled wine and 500 metres of festive paperchains and whole thing was a proper success and it made me very, very proud until the fire which destroyed the assembly hall, but that weren't my fault at all you can ask anyone.

DESCRIBE YOURSELF IN THREE WORDS?
Individual, hardworking, real.

FRIDAY 14TH AUGUST

No word back yet from the Working Magic employment thingy. This is bad 'cos the only way I've stopped my mother jarring my head was by telling her I'm sorted for a job alredy. OH BLOODY HELL! WHY DID I DO THAT??

I ain't a fake person me, swear to god, I'm ALWAYS keeping it real. But sometimes when my mother is getting all up in my face asking the same question over and over again like she's a Special Needs or something, which she isn't of course, she's just doing it on purpose to annoy me, well sometimes I just say whatever she wants to hear. Even if it's a total lie 'cos it makes her shut up.

So, today she goes 'So where you gonna work in London, Shiraz, eh? How you gonna make ends meet then? Eh? What you gonna do for money? You won't be getting hand-outs off me! You gonna live on fresh air then? 'Ere, what's gonna keep you fed and clothed? Eh? Eh?!' And in the end I shouts,

'I've got a job actually, Mother!'

'Eh? What kind?' she says, looking all shocked. So then I have to think proper fast and all I can think of is 'Estate Agency Office Clerk' as that's the job advert Danny was fiddling with in the window when I first spotted him and I was imagining ripping off his shirt and rolling about with him in a paddling pool of melted Galaxy truffle eggs.

'In an estate agent,' I says to my mother.

And she nearly chokes on her corned beef Breville toastie and goes, 'A what? What YOU gonna do in an estate agents?!'

So I panics a bit then says, 'I'm gonna help other people find homes to live in, of course.'

So, Mum thinks for a bit then she goes, ''Ere, like that woman Kirsteen Gossop on *Find Me a Home Fast* on ITV2? Her who takes folk to lots of houses and they never like one right till the last five minutes, then they do?'

And I says, 'Yeah, exactly like Kirsteen Gossop'

And Mum thinks for a bit then says, 'Ooh I like her I do, she always has lovely shoes.'

And I SHOULD have said, 'Nah, hang on Mother, actually, I'm kidding, I ain't really an estate agent at all.' But by this point she was looking quite happy and even a bit proud of me so I didn't say anything else and she stopped making a noise like a bloody fire alarm and we both sat there drinking our tea together looking happy but secretly only one of us was happy, 'cos I'd just told a big fat lie!

SATURDAY 15TH AUGUST

Oh God. My mother has told Nan, Cava-Sue, Murphy, Dad, Lewis, Aunty Glo, Mrs Rema and Bert at 89 that I'm going to be an estate agent. Mum's also told Sheila from the Prudential who comes to get her insurance money, Mr Khan who runs Costcutters and Wesley Barrington Bains II's mother who she bumped into when she was out getting scratch-cards. Oh bloody hell. And now I just got a text off my Wesley what said:

'Shizz. Just heard about the estate agent job. Well mint, innit. WBBXXXX'

Oh my days, now I feel more gulity than ever. I am under serious pressure.

GOOD NEWS!! Well in the end, anyways.

So, after four days of bricking it I ring Working Magic to say, 'Oi bruv did you get my form or what?'

And this African sounding woman answers and she says, all snooty like, 'Yes Miss Wood, I received your form over a week ago and it was very interesting but we have nothing for your type of person now, I'm afraid.'

So I says, 'Erm, so when do you think you will?'

And she says, 'Truthfully, you would be better to focus your job-seeking attentions elsewhere.' Then she goes totally silent.

So I says, 'What does that mean?' and she just tuts and says she's 'can't waste time on this call right now.'

So I feel my eyes go all prickly then and I go, 'Look, can I speak to Danny from Bolton?'

And she tuts again and says, 'You can leave Mr Jacobs a voicemail if you must. He's on the other line.' Then she cut me off without saying goodbye which was proper RUDE, then Danny's voicemessage cut in and it sounded so friendly I almost started crying, like a right DONUT.

So, I goes, 'Oi Danny, it's Shiraz can you give me a bell please?' Then my voice went all crackly and I tried to erase the voicemail 'cos I sounded pathetic but I couldn't work the touchtone button bloody stupid system, then I hung up and lay on my bed with my arms wrapped round my trackie bottom feeling as crap as I did the time Mrs

Fallow implied I was 'a chav from the estate'. That was the time I cried on the bus to my nan's house afterwards, and I told Nan I just had sore eyes.

So I'm lying there on the bed thinking there is no way Danny will ring me back . . . but then my phone rings AND IT"S HIM!!! Danny from Working Magic!!! Hoo-bloody-ray!!

Danny says that he didn't even know my application form was sitting in Angeliqua's in-tray. Danny says just to ignore Angeliqua as she can be a bit 'serious'. Danny says my application form really made him laugh as he could totally see I was being 'ironic'. Danny says he's got a job for me that begins on Tuesday September 8th in the head office of a famous international food company!

Ha ha ha ha ha ha ha ha ha!!! I am saved!!!!!!!!!!!!!!!!!!!

I just called Carrie and told her the news! Then I called my Wesley and asked if he could give me a lift to Whitechapel in his banana yellow golf on Sunday 30th August! I ain't got that much stuff anyhow. Not like Carrie. Her dad is bringing her stuff in a transit van with a roof rack. Wesley just sighed when I asked him and said 'No bother Shizza, whatever you want.'

So now it's official. Shiraz Bailey Wood is working and living in LONDON! WOOT WOOOT WOOOOOOOOOOOT! LMAO. ROFL. LULZZZZZZZZZZZZZZZZZZZZ!

11pm – What did Danny mean by 'ironic'?

SEPTEMBER

TUESDAY 1ST SEPTEMBER

10pm – Whitechapel – East London.

I think I should write down everything what's been happening over the last few days 'cos it's going to be a well important chapter in my autobiography when I am famous, 'cos it was the time I left home.

And not 'left home' like I did when I was little and my mother did my head in and I used to pack some spare knickers and some Rocky Robin biscuits in a plastic bag then storm out of our house banging the door, then an hour later come home again 'cos it was proper Baltic in the park and I'd eaten all the Rocky Robins. No. This was proper leaving home. I'm writing this from my new flat!!!

I'm in 10a Paramount Mansions. In my new bedroom! It's pretty much the same size as my old bedroom except I don't have bloody Murphy snortling through his *Zoo* magazine bikini-special making a noise like a pig eating porridge next door.

Me and Carrie have been dossing about in the lounge all night watching *EastEnders* and drinking loads of tea and eating Hobnobs and laughing like nutbags. 'Cos right now everything feels funny and a bit scary, in fact to tell you the truth my stomach feels all squishy and buzzing 24/7.

So anyways, I woke up well early on Sunday morning 'cos Wesley Barrington Bains II texted me at 8am, seeing if I still wanted a lift. Proper cold his message was too, by the way. LIFT INNIT? That's all it said. No kisses, no hello, no goodbye, no nothing. I felt like getting proper lairy with him to be honest 'cos I have just about had it with Wesley's negative vibes about my new life so I wanted to write back OI BRUV, LESS OF THE 'TUDE! But I didn't 'cos I didn't want to have to get the train.

And to be honest I don't like arguing with my Wesley. Wesley ain't really an arguing sort of person. His voice never goes loud and shouty. Not like my voice. I get shouty a lot. But the thing is, you see, everyone in my family likes shouting. And when there's like five of you shouting in a house and a dog blowing off all the time and Cava-Sue playing her emo music then you have to shout even louder to make yourself heard. But Wesley's house ain't like that. He grew up in a house just with his mum and everything is quite chilled and no one ever shouts at all. They just go all quiet and get the hump instead.

Anyways Wesley had the hump today. Wesley said he didn't have the hump but I could tell he did just by the way his shoulders were all hunched in his Ralph Lauren Polo jumper and the way he kept saying 'Shiraz' with a proper definite Z on the end. That's how he was saying my name today when he came to Thundersley Road and moved my little foldaway desk and my posh Anglepoise lamp from Habitat that he bought me last Christmas. And all my trainers. And my *High School Musical* duvet with Zac Efron's face on it what Carrie bought me as a joke but I use 'cos I love it to bits. And my jewellery box of Claire's Accessories hoops and scrunchies and all my books like *Jane Eyre* and *King Lear* and those rollerblades that I once bought 'second hand' off Clinton Brunton-Fletcher for a tenner and only used once 'cos I nearly killed myself outside Kebabish trying to take our Penny for a walk 'cos the fat thing took off running after a bloke who'd just bought a lamb shish and nearly dragged me under an ice-cream van like something Steve-O from *Jackass* would do.

And believe me this was in no way as funny as it sounds. I was well scared. Sometimes Penny is a right nightmare to take out. All she thinks about is her big fat belly. Silly fat Pen with her stupid snoring and her wind problem. I don't know why I'm missing her so much.

So anyways, me and Wesley packs everything into his banana-yellow Golf. And everything seems to be taking twice as long as it should 'cos Wesley is going proper slow time and pulling a sad face. So I says, 'Look, what is up with your face, bruv?' And Wesley just shrugs and says, 'Nothing.' And I says, 'Oh don't be daft Wesley, there is!' Then Wesley goes, 'I'm worried about you, that's what.' And I says, 'Why?' and Wesley says, 'Well, you're moving to Whitechapel in London, innit! It's a dodgy area! There's loads of mosques there. It's the centre of the Islamic community, innit? You'll get yourself blown up by those Al Qaeda, innit?'

So I starts laughing then and says, 'Wesley! It ain't that dodgy! *Essex* is dodgy! Someone got murked in Superkebab in Ilford last night! Clinton Brunton-Fletcher is selling drugs out of his house and all sorts of hoods he met in Juvenile Unit are coming by to buy 'em. And anyway what are Al Qaeda going to blow up a mosque for? I'm probably safer living beside a mosque than anywhere else in Britain you PLANTPOT.'

So Wesley tuts and says, 'Well, Whitechapel is where that Jack the Ripper murderer geezer used to live too, innit? And he killed loads of women! My mum used to collect the magazine about him! It came in parts every week and you made it into a folder, innit.'

So I just sighs at Wesley and says, 'Wes, Jack the Ripper was alive like a hundred years ago.' But Wes just shurgs and says, 'Well the police still ain't caught him though, innit?' Then we stood by his Golf not saying much for a long time, just staring at each other. And eventually Wes says, 'London is proper dangerous Shiraz, innit.' And I looked at him with his big lovely kind eyes and his bottom lip wobbling a bit and I wanted to put my arms around his body and cuddle him into me and kiss his ear and smell the Kouros aftershave on his neck but I knew that would just make things worse 'cos that would make

Wesley think even more that I should stay in Goodmayes for ever and that's the one thing I know I DON'T want.

Then my mother comes out of the house with a plate covered in tinfoil going "Ere Shiraz, I've done you some Findus Crispy Pancakes. They're the cheese and bacon ones, You might want them later if all you can buy is curry.' Then Nan and Clement came out and Nan gives me a big kiss and she did that clever Nan thing she does when she manages to stick an envelope in the back of my jeans pocket when my mum's not looking. And I looks later and it was a hundred quid!! Then Clement starts telling me about this proper legendary bagel shop just off Brick Lane in East London that is open day and night what sells fresh salmon and cream cheese bagels. And then Dad and Murphy come out the house and stand there with their arms folded not saying anything 'cos they're not really huggy, kissy saying goodbye sort of blokes.

'Laters Shiz,' said Murph, sort of kicking the tyre of Wesley's car like he was embarrassed to be being so mushy, which he totally wasn't.

'Oi! Take it easy now,' said my dad. 'And give your mother a ring soon and tell us how you're doing.'

'Yeah,' I said.

But then Cava-Sue comes out going, 'Oooh I am sorry Shiz! I nearly missed you! I was on the lav! I can't stop weeing today! Ooh this baby is kicking my bladder!! Anyway, come here and let me kiss you!' Then Cava-Sue grabs me and gives me a big cuddle but obviously there was a big lump blocking us. In fact she reminded me of that time Uma Brunton-Fletcher got caught thieving in Aldi one Christmas with a ten-pound turkey stuffed up her Jane Norman minidress.

So we all stood for a bit looking awkward. It weren't like goodbye on telly when folk always have something well meaningful to say just to finish things off. We aren't like folk off telly. We had nothing to say at all. Then I got in the front seat of the car and Mum bangs on the window and says, 'Ere Shiraz, when am I gonna see you next?!'

So I winds the window down but that's when Cava-Sue goes, 'Well she's coming home on November the fourteenth isn't she? To be with me while I give birth!'

Now, OK, I do sort of remember saying this a long time ago. But I thought Cava-Sue had forgotten.

'What?' says my mother. 'Is Shiraz coming to the hospital with you and Lewis? How will she get time off at the estate agents?'

But Cava-Sue just laughs and says, 'Oh I'm not having this baby in a hospital, Mother, I'm having it at home! In our living room!'

So my mother's face goes all purple then like a Ribenaberry and she shouts, 'You what? You can't have a baby in the living room, Cava-Sue. Are you off your bloody rocker?!'

Then Cava-Sue starts shouting, 'No I'm not off my

rocker, Mother. I am opting for a home birth! I'm not having my baby exposed to a vast array of transviral airbound superbugs!'

So my mum yells, 'Oh bloody marvellous, Cava-Sue! Where you going to have it then? On my new rug what's just arrived from Littlewoods catalogue? I don't even let your father eat his curry near that rug!'

So Cava-Sue yells, 'No not on your precious rug, Mother. Lewis and I will be hiring a paddling pool. I'm having a water birth! And Shiraz will be helping because she's my little sister and I need some strong feminine figures around! And you can help too if you want!'

And right then I wound up the car window proper fast. And as we turned the corner of Thundersley Road I could still see everyone waving their arms around and arguing. My mum's hands were flapping like she was doing the actions to *YMCA*, while Cava-Sue was sort of pointing at her bump and waving her arms a bit like she was doing the Macarena. But by this point I was driving away from them all in the direction of London so I couldn't hear them shouting, which was really, really mint.

So the traffic was quite bad as we drove from Essex to London but eventually we gets to Paramount Mansions, which to be honest looked even more shady than the first time I saw it. A right big intimidating house it is, in the middle of a load of terraced houses. But I honestly don't care at all. And Carrie had already arrived and Barney has moved about fifty boxes of her stuff in. Carrie has basically brought the entire contents of her room in Draperville and that is LOADS OF STUFF 'cos Carrie is well spoilt. Carrie's dad has even bought her a new superslim Blackberry so that she can email and get Internet on the go too. And here's me with my pay-as-you-go Nokia that looks like it came free off the council.

So Carrie was on the sofa in our new living room with Dave Pearce's Dance Anthems on her digital radio, opening a packet of Chocolate Hobnobs and she goes, 'Fancy a cuppa?!'

So we had a cuppa and at some point Wesley left, which I don't really remember that much about 'cos I was trying on some of Carrie's dresses that she was unpacking. And then we sat by the living-room window looking over the quietish street of houses which are mostly flats and we played Carrie's Hed Kandi CDs and watched as hundreds of Muslim blokes in robes all made their way home from the mosque. And down the street some art students carrying tins of paint and brushes were on their way home. And then a load of quite lush looking lads arrived and started loading guitars and drums into a transit van near our house. And everyone looked proper interesting and different from each other, whereas in Essex everyone dresses the same. I've been thinking how mad everyone looks for the last few days as I've been wandering around getting totally lost.

Anyway tonight me and Carrie stayed in and sat on the

sofa with duvets around us, still surrounded by boxes 'cos we still haven't properly unpacked, chatting for hours and hours about life. I finally ate the Findus Crispy Pancakes that were in the fridge, cold, with salad cream on. And now I'm lying in bed, which feels all bumpy 'cos I think I've put the sheets on wrong and I'm wondering how I've managed to spend almost seventy pounds already on nothing and how the hell I'll survive 'cos it's all so EXPENSIVE here but I think I'll be OK, because soon I'm starting my new job.

My new job?

Oh my days, there goes my stomach again.

TUESDAY 8TH SEPTEMBER

Whitechapel – 10pm.

Started my first temp job today! At Sunshine Sandwiches Head Office near London Bridge right beside the River Thames! Danny at Working Magic has got me four weeks' work – 8.30am – 4.30pm – in the Customer Services department. My job is to 'ensure the clients get the maximum enjoyment out of their sandwich eating experience'. Well that's what Danny from Working Magic told me when he rang yesterday, but to be honest I weren't really listening properly 'cos I was imagining covering him in an entire pot of Body Shop Mango Body Butter and giving his bumcheeks one of those 'sensual massages' what they always go on about in Cava-Sue's *Marie Claire* magazine. Oh my life, Danny is bare CHOONG.

Anyway, when Danny told me about the job I felt a bit scared 'cos Lewis and Cava-Sue have both worked in the Sunshine Sandwiches shop in Ilford Mall and people are always dissing the food. Especially the Teryaki Chicken which to be quite frank tastes a lot like old hamster in bum gravy and OH MY DAYS I've got to stop saying stuff like that 'cos not everyone can handle me keeping it so real. Especially Martika the Customer Services manager who was training me today. She was bare grumpy like she was coming on her period or something. 'Cept I don't know if you still have periods when you're her age, 'cos she was like thirty-six or something PROPER ANCIENT.

So I says to Martika not to stress that I'll diss the food or nothing, 'cos I reckon the Italian Meatball sandwich ain't actually that minging. Y'know, if you put loads of ketchup satchets on it and totally forget about that weirdo Marco who used to work in the Ilford branch with our Cava-Sue who used to flick his bogies in the coleslaw and eventually got fired for trying to show the cleaner his willie. He was enough to put anyone off their six-inch Meatball Bonanza with special sauce for life believe me.

But Martika just stared at me when I said that. Then she said she was going for a fag, then she never came back. She just left me sitting by myself in a small office in the basement looking like a munter wearing Cava-Sue's old burgundy interview suit and this phone headset which totally kept catching on my hoop earrings.

And when I looked at the desk there was this massive ring binder full of notes with a sticker on the cover what said:

OFFICIAL GUIDELINES TO SUNSHINE SANDWICHES CUSTOMER HELPLINE COMPLAINTS

And it's about now that I starts remembering that bit on the side of the Sunshine Sandwich wrappers that always says:

HEY! DID THIS SANDWICH PUT SUNSHINE IN YOUR LIFE!? IF NOT CALL OUR SPECIAL SANDWICH EXPERTS ON 0800 800 9456 AND TELL US WHAT WE'RE DOING WRONG!

OMG! That's me!! I'm answering that phone! I'm the Special Sunshine Sandwich Expert!! Ha ha ha! What a laugh! I've spent all day listening to folk telling me about their wheat allergies or the consistency of the egg mayonnaise in Scunthorpe or how they've got tuna salad stuck round the back of their teeth brace! Then we have a bit of a chat and then I post them some vouchers to say sorry and, well . . . that's it!!!!!!

Today I gave out about four hundred quidsworth of vouchers. That seems like loads, but it's not like it's my money or nothing and Sunshine Sandwiches have got tons of cash so it's totally fine.

Ha ha ha ha! Eight pound an hour for chatting on the phone!!! I LOVE chatting on the phone! And the rest of the day I was texting Carrie who was well bored at Butterz Academy 'cos they were doing their 'Health and Safety' certificate so she just skived off to Prêt à Manger and had a mocha instead. Eight pound an hour! LMAO! I am going to be soooooo rich! I can't believe I nearly mugged myself off finishing those boring A-Levels.

And when I gets home tonight Carrie and me put on apricot facepacks that she stole from Butterz Academy and we ate Pot Noodles and sat about in dressing gowns in our own flat like laydeez of leisure!

12pm – Oh god. I've been meaning to ring Wesley for days to thank him properly for the lift and everything but I've totally forgot again.

THURSDAY 10TH SEPTEMBER

Today wasn't that much fun really. It took me an hour and a half to get to work because the bus was in a big jam on Blackfriars Bridge and then when I got there Martika started jarring my head BIG TIME.

It was only 9 o'clock! I told her that it weren't my fault but she just tutted and said, 'Punctuality is very important at Sunshine Sandwiches! Imagine if the customers lose confidence in our brand and start dining elsewhere?!'

So I says to Martika, ''Ere love that won't be 'cos of my timekeeping, that'll be 'cos people keep finding pubes in the Cheese and Pickle baguettes!' Then I showed Martika my notepad from yesterday with CURLY PUBE/ SCUNTHORPE/CHEESE AND PICKLE?? written on it and then her face went light turquoise and she went for another Lambert and Butler Superking out by the wheelie bins where all the pigeons crap.

Today seemed to last longer than yesterday. I got the bus home and it goes over London Bridge but I couldn't see much of the view as it was so packed I had my face pressed into someone's gym kit bag. And considering I've sat in an office in a basement all day that's the only thing I've really seen today.

Me and Carrie are totally over Pot Noodles now. Tonight we had Nice and Spicy NikNaks with Muller Rice for pudding.

From – kingmurphyisthegreatest@bullfrogbroadband.co.uk
To – theshizz@wideblueyonder.co.uk
Date – Saturday 12th September.

Oi Shizzlebizzle! Wa g'wan sista!!!? Just thought I'd say the House is proper amazing without you. Ha ha lmao!!! Mum has finally fessed up that I am her favourite kid and you iz the one who was adopted off the pikeys. Sozzzz about that Shiz. Anywayzzz I just wanted to say that we iz all OK in Goodmayes. Oh and Penny is proper slim now and well clever like a police dog (yeah, right). Cava-Sue is getting bigger every day like she is gonna explode any minute! Can't believe that you are coming to help with the birth. DISGUSTING MAN. I am going to Vue instead to watch a movie until it is all over. Oh and THE PADDLING POOL ARRIVED FROM ARGOS YESTERDAY!!! HA HA HA. C YA – WOULDN' WANNABEYA! Your little bruvvaMURPHYXXXXX PS – CAN I COME AND SEE YOU IN LONDON SHIZ? I CAN COME ANY SATURDAY. WRITEBACKSOON RIGHT???

MONDAY 14TH SEPTEMBER

Oh my days. I am totally in trouble at Sunshine Sandwiches. So today Martika comes in to the basement at 8.45 just as I was sitting down and she's got one of those total face-of-fury looks on, a bit like Carrie's mum's face when she found that Alexis the chihuahua had wiped her bum right along the cream stair carpet in a sort of turbo skidmark. In other words, LIVID.

So I says, 'I'm only fifteen minutes late!' And she says, 'It's not that Shiraz! Have you been giving Sunshine Sandwich vouchers to all the customers?!' So I says 'Course I have! The phone's been ringing off the hook all week! The sandwiches are wack!' And Martika goes, 'You're not supposed to just give vouchers out willy-nilly! You're supposed to talk to the customer for a while and see if you can come to a verbal agreement first!'

So I says, 'What's that supposed to mean?' And she says, 'Well most of the time customers just want to get a problem off their chest! You can't just throw money at them all! You've given out over £1,800 worth of vouchers since you arrived! That wasn't in your training!'

So I gets a bit angry then and I says, ''Ere, you haven't given me no training! You've never had a Lambert and Butler out your gob for three days.' And Martika cringed a bit and said, 'That's not true!' So I goes, 'Yeah it is! The front of your hair has got a yellow streak! And I don't know whether it's fag smoke, soot or pigeon crap!' Well, Martika went mental then and shouted, 'That is totally bloody unacceptable language! I'm going to speak to my manager about you! Get on with your work and don't give out another single voucher!'

The rest of the day seemed to last for ages.

Martika isn't keeping it real at all. OF COURSE PEOPLE WANT THE VOUCHERS! If you don't give them out people just moan on and on and on! I wasn't very patient with some of them. Tonight I walked home along the side of the Thames just to see some of London, 'cos I've hardly done anything at all but work and sleep since I arrived.

Mum rang tonight to see how the estate agency is going. I nearly spat out my Marmite toastie then. I said it wasn't as easy as Kirsteen Gossop on telly made it look. But I've still managed to sell a few 'condos'. So then Mum asked me what a 'condo' was. I don't know what a bloody condo is. It's just something Seth and Summer talk about on *The OC*.

TUESDAY 15TH SEPTEMBER

Dear Nan and Clement,
Having a lovely time in London! Me
and Carrie have really settled
into our new flat and we are very
happy. I am WELL LOVING my new
career as an estate agent and the
money is proper good and
everything here is sorted and
amazing. Today me and Carrie
are going to go sightseeing to
Buckingham Palace and then
tonight we will probably go and
see a famous show like Joseph
and his Amazing Technicoloured
Dreamcoat and then go for food
at the Hard Rock Café or
something. Please don't worry
about me as I am totally fine and
happy and not homesick at all.
Lots of Love your
Granddaughter Shiraz x xxx
Ps — Just to say that the
address is 10a Paramount
Mansions, just in case you want to
send me any more cash or
anything, although obviously you
don't need to 'cos, as I say,
I'm OK.

Mr and Mrs C
  Carrington,
19 Wilmslow Gardens,
Chadwell Heath,
Essex,
RM6 5BU

Well today was a right bloody joke. So I gets to work at 8.26am – ON TIME MARTIKA THANK YOU VERY MUCH! STICK THAT UP YOUR MIMSY SIDEWAYS! – and I'm feeling well proud of myself 'cos I've even managed to iron my hoodie and find a pair of tights without ladders and put some *J-Lo Glow* perfume on and everything. And I'm thinking, actually, this working for a living lark isn't actually so bad after all, but that's 'cos I've not taken any calls yet and I've totally forgotten what a bunch of complete and utter BUM WINNETS the British general public really are.

So first call I get is from this proper hoity-toity posh woman in Hastings and she says, 'Ooh good day to you, I'm calling about an Edam and sundried tomato sandwich what I have purchased from your boutique beside the railway station. I always buy lunch on my way to work to save time later. But the one I've bought today looks a bit stale!' So I sort of snorts a bit 'cos I'm trying not to laugh and I says, 'Well why did you buy it if it looks stale?' So she says, 'Because Edam is the only sandwich made with rye bread. I have a serious wheat allergy you know?!'

So I tuts a bit and say, 'Oh my life! Another wheat allergy?' 'Cos I've had it up to my back teeth with hearing about wheat allergies. That's all folk moan on about all day – BLOODY WHEAT ALLERGIES – and I feel like saying, 'Bruv, what you doing in a sandwich shop then you nutbag! Bread is wheat! Get yerself down the chippy! Have a pickled egg!'

Well anyway, wheat-allergy woman didn't like me giggling at her and she says, 'Is something funny? I don't find my allergy amusing! My stomach swells up like a balloon and I get excessively gassy!' Well this makes me laugh properly now 'cos her voice was all high-pitched when she said it, like she was holding in a big fart with both her bumcheeks proper tight right then. So I goes, 'Well we do ham on rye bread! Why didn't you get that!?'

So posh wheat-fart woman cries, 'I'm a vegetarian! And I wouldn't eat ham anyway as I've got an intolerance to processed foods!' So then I start howling with laughter going, 'Bloody hell you're a right one-woman party you are! You've got less dinner options than my nan when our Staffy steals her bottom dentures and buries them in the garden! And she can't eat nothing but Cup-a-soups for a week!'

But wheat-fart woman didn't think this was jokes at all. 'I don't think you're taking my illnesses very seriously!' she shouts, so I tries to stop laughing and I say, 'Look, I am being serious, I just find it a bit funny how all you snooty rich folk who could afford to eat whatever you want have got all these allergies and intolerances! Then all those poor folk in Africa whose heads are proper big and their bodies are like skeletons and they're covered in flies and look all minging and that, well they'll eat anything won't they? Those African geezers don't go, "Ooh please, rich people, please send us some food! Only nothing with meat or wheat 'cos we're allergic!" Do they? No, those poor gits would have your hand off for a ham poonani!' And it's not like I was being rude to her, I was only being real. Some people can't handle me being so real.

So wheat-fart woman, who is crying now, I'm not sure why, maybe she was in a small phone box and one of her gassy farts had escaped or something, says, 'What has this got to do with Africa?' And I says, 'Erm, I'm not really sure.' 'Cos sometimes when I'm ranting I totally lose my train of thought. But the important thing was I kept arguing until she hung up and I didn't give her no free vouchers!!

And then Martika came storming in and said she'd been monitoring my progress on another line, and being so rude to the customers was a sackable offence and then she put all of the things on my desk into a box and made Caspos the security guard escort me out of the back door, carrying the box. Then they threw me OUT!!!!!!!!!!

I am unemployed! And I've only got forty five quid left of Nan's money! And all the rest of the money I saved up from Mr Yolk is going on next month's rent and Cheese Strings and Wotsits. WHAT AM I GOING TO DO???!!!!!

SATURDAY 19TH SEPTEMBER

Carrie reckons I've got to chill my boots about this whole work/money thing. Carrie reckons I can't let myself get all stressed 'cos stress gives you wrinkles and wrinkles are ugly and ugly people aren't happy 'cos no one butterz is happy are they?

Carrie wasn't really helping with my stress levels at this point as she was lying on the carpet in our living room with her ankles in the air waxing her own bikini line! Carrie has been doing 'hair removal' this week at Butterz. So basically she spent the whole morning glueing strips of paper to the inside of her thighs, then shouting ''Ere, Shizzle? Shout one-two-three!' So I'd do that and on 'three' she'd go 'Rrrrrrrrrip!' with the strip, then screams a proper disgusting loud swear word, then she'd show me the strip with all the pubes on looking like a disgusting hairy mutant Shredded Wheat and we'd both laugh until we nearly wet ourselves. We'd never do this type of thing at home in Goodmayes. Here we can sort of do whatever we want.

So after Carrie had given herself a ladygarden what looked like a bald man's head with a small Mohican, we went to the greasy spoon café Star Bar on the corner of Paramount Road and had full English breakfast with double bubble and squeak and loads of tomato sauce. Carrie wouldn't let me pay for mine seeing as I am totally unemployed. She's proper sweet like that is Carrie.

Then Carrie starts banging on about how it's Saturday night tonight and we're not being miserable cows 'cos we're going to a party. Carrie says one of the best things about being a Butterz Beauty Academy student is that the students get put on the guestlists for loads of cool parties.

I reckon this is mainly 'cos all the girls on Carrie's course are tall and blonde and slinky and look like birds off *Hollyoaks*. In fact totally the opposite to me, who is small and brunette and wobbly and looks more like something off of *Battlestar Gallactica* that they might find on a haunted planet and shout, 'Oh my god captain! It's a monster! Blast it with a stungun!'

So I says that to Carrie and she says 'Oh shut up' and anyways she's giving me a makeover and turning me into a whole new Shiraz. I liked the sound of that 'cos right then I wasn't much of a fan of the old Shiraz with her stupid big gob that had made the woman with the wheat intolerance cry in a phone box. 'Well Carrie I ain't got any money for drinks or nothing,' I says. 'Not a problem!' Carrie says. 'Everything will be free 'cos this is a "launch party".'

I didn't know what a 'launch party' was so Carrie said that basically a big American make-up company were bringing out a new lip-gloss this week and this was a special party to celebrate. So that meant we'd get a free lip-gloss at the end of the party to take home! And the drinks would be totally free too. Well I couldn't believe what I was hearing! 'All the drinks are free?' I kept saying.

'How? How? How can the drinks be free!?' 'Well the make-up company pays the bill!' says Carrie. 'All these posh parties are free!'

Well I couldn't get my nut around this at all. Because if Goodmayes Social in Essex all of a sudden said, 'Come down on Saturday night and the drinks are all free!' well, believe me, some geezers would still be there on Sunday night. And some folk would stay drinking till they at least wet their pants standing by the bar and probably at least one person would die of alcohol poisoning. People in London are just a lot more classy. It's a fact.

So Carrie gave me one of her black dresses with a sort of V-shaped neckline and flarey miniskirt and some long black boots to my knee and then she put my make-up on with sponges and brushes the posh way like you see models on telly getting it done. She started with foundation and made all my zits totally disappear then she made my eyes all smoky with eyeshadow and mascara and then she drew my lips in with lip pencil. And I don't know how the hell Carrie does make-up so good 'cos whenever she does me I look almost buff! Then whenever *I* try to do my make-up like this I end up looking like when our Murphy joined the army cadets and he used to paint camouflage stripes on and hide in bushes.

So when Carrie had finished I looked in the mirror and I felt proper chuffed. We got our bags and went off to get the bus to the party and the lush lads in the flat down Paramount Road who are always carrying instruments came to their window and wolf-whistled us and my heart started beating proper fast.

The lip-gloss party was at this place called the Takiikii Club beside the River Thames. It was totally posh and I kept thinking someone would stop us when we were in the guestlist queue and say, 'Shiraz Bailey Wood from Superchav Academy! You are too pikey to be here' but no one did. In fact no one looked at us at all. In fact now and then in London you feel proper invisible like you're a ghost.

So we arrives at about 8.30pm. The party was already proper full. And it was bare exciting 'cos honest to god, these had to be some of the most buff people I have ever seen in real life ever! Everyone was tall and slim and all the women had really toned upper arms and no bingo-wings and designer dresses and their eyebrows plucked into neat arches and high heels like Victoria Beckham wears. And all the boys looked proper rich and like they worked out at the gym and they all had tanned skin and clean fresh clothes on and no one had an England football shirt on or tattoos on their face or a hoodie or even trainers!!!

And everyone was drinking these weird posh drinks which were sort of orange coloured with fruit floating in them called 'Mandarin and Kumquat Martinis'. And a model in a white bikini was walking about with trays of them giving them out for free! So me and Carrie took one and sat down at a table and I picked up a cocktail menu and I saw that a Martini like that actually cost sixteen pound fifty!!!!!!

Sixteen fifty for one tiny drink!! That's the same as it costs for a posh dress from New Look! Or an entire bag of potato waffles and chicken wings and oven chips in Iceland! Or all my bus and tube fares in London for about a week!!! And when I looked at the bar snacks menu they had squid tempura for twenty-two quid! And satay chicken for eighteen quid! What's that all about? Who can afford to have a snack for eighteen quid!!! And after about half an hour the door flew open and this crowd of skinny pretty girls came in that were about the same age as me and Carrie. And one girl with silky brown hair was talking loudly into her mobile phone going, 'Yah! Yah! I know! I've got a car waiting outside to take me there! I'll be like half an hour! Yeah! I'm showing face here for a bit then I'll get my driver to find you!'

Well, I thought Carrie was going to wet her knickers with excitement. 'Shiraz! It's Kitten Montague-Jones!!' she says. And I'm like 'Who?' and Carrie's like 'Kitten Montague-Jones! Her dad is that famous rock star Animal Jones who used to be in The Ghosttown Rodents! She writes a column for *London Alive* newspaper called Kitten's Titbits! She's like bare famous! Kitten Montague-Jones!? KITTEN MON-TA-GUE-JONES!!!!!? She always says "Mwah mwah dahlinks!" That's her catchphrase? And "Love you madly smittenkittens!" C'mon Shiz you know who I mean?'

Well, to be honest by this point everyone knew her 'cos Carrie was saying it so loud that Kitten actually turned around and looked at us like we were stale poos floating in a public loo. Then Kitten says into her mobile phone, 'Oh believe me, I won't be staying long, it's a bit chavtastic in here. I'm going to see if there's a VIP section to stand in!' And then she wanders off into a bit of the party we weren't allowed into because we weren't on the VIP guestlist. Well Carrie was nearly melting with happiness. And I goes, 'So what does Kitten actually do?!' and Carrie says, 'Oh nothing really. Her dad is like a millionaire. She just goes to parties really! Isn't she amazing!' To be honest, I didn't really think she was. She seemed right up herself. What makes *her* a Very Important Person?

Anyway then me and Carrie starts laughing about having a dad called 'Animal' and we had another Kumquat Martini and the DJ played some Justin Timberlake and we were dancing and giggling and we met some posh blokes from Putney and we ate some squid tempura stuff which was basically chewy fish that gives you heartburn and we went home on the midnight nightbus and when I got home my head was all dizzy and rushing and I thought OH MY LIFE that was probably the best party I've ever been to in the history of the world EVER. END OF.

And at about 1am Wesley Barrington Bains II sent me a text saying U OK INNIT?? So I texted him back saying

HAVING THE MINTEST TIME EVAAAAA!!. And I thought he might want to chat, but he never texted after that.

He must have went to sleep.

MONDAY 21ST SEPTEMBER

34, Thundersley Road
Goodmayes
Essex
IG5 2XS

Dear Shiraz
Just a few lines to see how you're getting on. I've left umpteen messages on that phone of yours but I've heard nothing. I get all my news second hand from Barney Draper! I hear Carrie is top of her class at that beauty school! Anyway, I know you don't always have credit token things on your phone so I've put a tenner in with this letter so you can top it up and ring me! It wouldn't hurt you y'know? I don't like to nag you, you know I don't Shiraz, but Mrs Reema down our road's daughter manages to give her mother a bell most nights and she lives in bleeding Pakistan!! Anyway Shiraz, I hope your job is going well. I always think of you when I am watching my programmes. What estate agency are you working at Shiraz? I rung a few up on the main street in Whitechapel the other day

and none of them had heard of you. Ain't London proper unfriendly? No one even bothers to learn your name down there do they? Anyway, got to fly now as I'm taking Penny to the vet's to have her bum looked at. It's all red again. Could be piles I reckon. PLEASE RING US! All my love – Mum xxx

Oh my days, I NEED another job. I am skint. Carrie just caught me with my head stuffed down the back of the sofa searching for 'lost treasure'. She's lent me another tenner.

Thing is, I keep on ringing about jobs I see in the back of *London Alive* but they've already been taken by Polish people with degrees in Maths who can speak like four languages. And today I says to one of the blokes I rung, 'Yeah but I speak English, blud!' And he goes, 'Yes, but most of my Polish employees speak it better than you.' 'Yeah bare jokes, bruv, whatever, jog on,' I said.

And to make things WORSE, folk keep asking me for 'a reference' which is a note off your last boss saying how amazing you are. Well I rang Martika at Sunshine Sandwiches and asked but I probably won't be showing anyone what she sent.

By the way Martika, you didn't eject me from the building!!! I WANTED TO GO ANYWAY TO GET AWAY FROM YOUR STINKY YELLOW NICOTINE CLAWS OF DOOM FINGERS!!!!

I rang Danny at Working Magic today to see if he'd give me another chance at the agency. He sort of laughed for a bit, then eventually he said I should come in on Thursday when Angeliqua's got a day off. Thank you Danny!!!!!

THURSDAY 24TH SEPTEMBER

Oh my life! I love Danny at Working Magic! So I get there today and he's sitting at his desk wearing a black T-shirt and navy blue jeans talking on the phone. So I sat and watched him for a while and I'm thinking, 'Jeezlouise, dat boy just look chooong from every single bloody angle. Like there is no way you could ever look butterz.' Not like my Wesley who only really looks buff when he's had a shave and got a fresh shirt on but the rest of the time he's got manboobs and a face like a dropped pie.

So I sits down and Danny just laughs and says 'Well Shiraz, you were certainly a hit at Sunshine Sandwiches.' So I sort of groans and goes 'Mmnnnnnnmmyeahsorry.' Then he goes, 'Well what do you think went wrong?' So I looks at him and before I knew it I was wittering on about how I really really tried but the thing is I came to London to SEE London NOT to sit in a cellar with nothing to see at all. In fact nothing to see but a massive talking cigarette in a frumpy Etam business suit with turbo dandruff – YES I MEAN YOU, MARTIKA.

So I says to Danny, 'Look I can't help it if I always keep it real? I can't help it if I always say things exactly as I see it? And what was I supposed to do when that woman found the ginger pube in her cheese and pickle sandwich? Send her some of my own so she could start a collection!!!? Send her some of my best mate Carrie's? Well I can't mate, she ain't got none left!!!'

Well Danny nearly sprayed coffee all over his computer screen when I said that. Then he opened up his packed lunch and said, 'Do you want a KitKat, Shiraz?' And I said, 'Yes, please, Danny' because all I'd had for breakfast was a mouthful of fluff from down the back of the sofa when I was looking for my bus fare.

'You, Shiraz Bailey Wood, are a total one-off,' Danny says to me, shaking his head, while tapping away on his computer. 'Thank you very much,' I says.

Danny laughed a bit more. 'Y'know something? It's a good job I like you!' he says, then he pulled some paper out of the printer and stuck it in my hand. 'Here!' he says. 'This is a job with a lovely view of London. And there's going to be a lot of keeping it real involved so it's perfect for you. Don't mess this one up!'

So I looked at the bit of paper ... and it was only like the best job ever!

Shiraz Bailey Wood is back in business!!!!!!!!!!!!!!!!!!

11.15pm – Hang on. Did Danny Jacobs from Working Magic say that he liked me????

I'm sure he just means as a friend. He must do. OMG.

OCTOBER

THURSDAY 1ST OCTOBER

Now, get ready for this . . . I, Shiraz Bailey Wood, am a 'ride supervisor' on the London Eye in London! The London Eye! One of the most famous tourist attractions IN THE WORLD EVER!

Ooh, by the way, if this diary is being read in, like, the year 2105 by boffins in spacesuits who've dug it up in a time capsule and don't know what the London Eye is, well it is like this MASSIVE BIG WHEEL in London right beside the River Thames. It's a bit like the one you get at Thurrock Fair on Bank Holiday Monday. But much much much bigger and better! Plus you don't get your phone jacked by rudes at the London Eye, like you always do at Thurrock Fair, either. And you don't win a half-dead goldfish.

So anyway, the London Eye is this gigantic steel wheel which has these things called pods on it where people stand inside. Then the wheel spins round very slowly giving everyone inside a 'magnificent panoramic view of London'!

Panoramic means you can see everything! Like from every angle. A bit like when Latoya Bell wears a miniskirt with no thong. Except this view doesn't make you want to bleach your eyeballs. Anyways, my job is to help all the tourists get on and get off their pod again. And I go up in the pods and make people's thirty-minute journey more 'comfortable' by telling them interesting facts about London. The supervisor lady who met me on my first day, Jayne Deacon, double-checked I knew a bit about London and I said, 'Yeah, course I do, I'm from Essex! I know the big smoke like the back of my hand!'

Well, she looked proper pleased at that and signed me up for loads of shifts which was amazing as I am so skint right now that I've had Birdseye Fishcakes with mango chutney for my supper all week. They were the only two things in Somerfield's Out of Date section what almost went together. I didn't want to lie to Jayne Deacon but I need the cash!! The truth is I don't know ANYTHING about London.

I mean, yeah, I grew up nearby, but Mum never let us come to London when I was little 'cos it was 'too dirty' and 'too dear' and 'full of nutters and foreigners'. In fact, truth to tell, I'm always lost down here, looking at maps on bus stops, walking the wrong way down roads etbloodycetera.

In fact, Carrie says that she's getting me iron-on name-tags with my address on like we had in Primary One and sticking them in all my hoodies and thongs so at least if the police find me in Brixton wandering like a homeless they can deliver me back.

So, anyway, I MUST REMEMBER to learn some

interesting facts about London. Some stuff about Big Ben and the Houses of Parliament and Westminster Abbey and all that sort of stuff. I tried to read some stuff tonight on Carrie's Blackberry but it was proper dull so I watched *I'm a Celebrity Get Me Out of Here* instead. That Reuben Smart from *Fast-Track Family Feud* has got some balls, eating all those fried kangaroo anuses in the jungle.

I will TOTALLY ABSOLUTELY learn some facts this weekend DEFFO.

SATURDAY 3RD OCTOBER

I'M 18 TODAY!!!!! WOOT WOOT WOOT! BRAP BRAP BRAP! BIG UP SHIZZLEBIZZLE WOOD WHO IS PROPERLY AN ADULT!!! HA HA HA! TODAY IS MY BIRTHDAY!!!

SUNDAY 4TH OCTOBER

Oh my days! Yesterday was the most mint time ever! I'm in bed now trying to piece it all together, 'cos it gets a bit hazy in parts!!! Thing was, when I woke up I thought, 'Bloody hell I am totally meant to be a grown-up now!' and I felt proper STRESSED 'cos I thought, 'Oh no, what if I've started being all "mature" overnight and started liking minging American tan wrinkly tights and I start needing those Tena Lady Pad things for women who can't even laugh without widdling down their own legs? And what if I've started to look like those sad old women who you see down TopShop who are like thirty-three or something and they're trying on the new season range and you're like, "Mate, you are mugging yourself right off there with those skinny jeans, get yourself down M and S for a nice pair of elasticated-waist trousers!" ha ha ha.'

So, anyways, I looked in the bathroom mirror and PHEW I looked exactly the same. In fact, if anything I looked a bit better 'cos the fishcake/mango chutney diet is quite low in calories and I've been walking three miles a day to work so now my bum looks almost half as good as Carrie's. OK make that twenty per cent as good as Carrie's.

So then Carrie runs in my room with a birthday card and pressies!! She got me an amazing big pair of hoop earrings from Accessorise and a blue top from Mango which is PROPER MINT!! And Carrie was singing 'HAPPY BIRTHDAY TO YOU! HAPPY BIRTHDAY TO YOU! SHIRAZ BAILEY BAILEY WOOD I GOTTA BIG DAY PLANNED FOR YOU!!!' And right away I knew I was gonna be in trouble 'cos Carrie can't help but get us both into trouble. It is like in her genes or something, proper written all over her DNA molecule thingies.

Then the postman brought my other birthday cards!! One off Mum and Dad, one off Nan and Clement (BOTH WITH TENNERS IN!!) one off Uma and Zeus, one off Cava-Sue and Lewis and even one from our Murphy which was addressed to 'Miss Shiraz Moonmask' 'cos our Murphy always says I have a big face like the moon. And this used to make me cry when I was little but now it makes me laugh 'cos it is our own little joke and it's silly.

Oh and I also got a card off Wesley Barrington Bains II with a voucher for Hennes in it!! And he wrote a letter in it too but I didn't have time to read it 'cos I was too excited trying on my Mango top! And now I can't find it. I think it maybe went in the rubbish. Oh well, it probably was only a few lines. Wesley hates writing.

Anyway, then Carrie made us both get ready and we were out the house by 11.30am off on our big London adventure!! Carrie had printed a list off the Internet of all the things I am LEGALLY allowed to do now I'm eighteen years old! And we decided to try to do them all in one day!!! Ha ha ha! It was the best day ever!!

So first thing me and Carrie did was go into Mr Afzah's shop on the corner of Paramount Road and I LEGALLY bought a little miniature bottle of sherry for £1.76. Carrie and me chose sherry 'cos we figured it was the sort of sensible drink a grown-up would want. I mean let's face it you don't see many grown-ups drinking sherry then setting fire to a bus shelter, do you? Not like that Banana Red Mad Dog 20/20 stuff that actually made Chantalle Strong take her knickers off at Chenai Green's barbecue and whirl them round her head then throw them on the grill. MAN THAT STUFF IS EVIL. Anyway, it turns out sherry is minging, so we spat most of it away.

Mr Afzah just looked so depressed when he sold us it. I mean, in fairness we were two girls in short skirts and hoodies in his shop, in the morning, during Ramadan, demanding alcohol. And Mr Afzah is a Muslim geezer who don't drink booze and prays five times a day, whose own daughter wears a head to toe niqab with just an eye slit and mouth slit so he's bound to find us a bit shocking. Mr Afzah's a nice bloke though. When Carrie orders shoes and stuff from the catalogue and it arrives when she's at work he takes it in his shop and puts the card through the door. It's OK living amongst all these Islamic dudes as they're well chilled out. It's weird 'cos they're nothing like the ones on Sky News who are always wishing a plague on people's houses and burning stuff.

And Mr Afzah's daughter is nice too, but blimey she's a real big girl. Always pushing Maltesers through the mouth slot in her niqab she is. It's daft really 'cos Minstrels would fit better. Anyways, I reckon she must be having a right old struggle during Ramadan when she can't eat from like 6am till 7pm. I wonder if she hides stuff under her niqab so Allah can't see? A Domino pizza or something.

Anyways, then we went to Star Bar Café and got egg and chips and planned to have more amazing eighteenth birthday adventures. We borrowed Anton from Star café's *Whitechapel Gazette* 'cos we wanted to find out about any elections, 'cos I am now old enough to VOTE!!! But there weren't any elections on a Saturday, so then we went to

Corals betting shop to put on MY FIRST BET instead!!

Me and Carrie put a quid each way on a horse at 'ten to one' odds called Mint Lass running in the 2.15 at Carlisle! And we didn't have a Scooby Doo what 'ten to one' was and we didn't even know where Carlisle was and we weren't even sure whether Mint Lass was a greyhound or a horse or donkey but IT DIDN'T MATTER 'cos we were so busy wetting ourselves at this builder leaning over the counter putting a bet on who had the BIGGEST DEEPEST HAIRIEST BUM CLEAVAGE EVER STICKING OUT OF HIS JEANS! And as we were walking out Carrie stuffed a small betting shop pen down the back of his undies and he NEVER EVEN NOTICED and when we ran out of the shop I had to hold on to the side of a parked car for a while 'cos I was laughing so loud I could hardly stand up!!!

So after that we got the Northern Line tube to Camden Town in north west London which is where all the emos and the indie and the nu-metal and the nu-rave kids hang out 'cos there's a market and tonnes of bars and stuff to do etc. Everyone in the market looked a lot like my Cava-Sue and her Lewis all with floppy hair dyed black, looking all proper miserable, like they've just heard their cat's got AIDS or something.

Then me and Carrie went to a bar – which I am LEGALLY allowed to do now – although Carrie couldn't drink yet – but I had a blue WKD and we were talking to loads of strangers and telling them it was my birthday!

And people were buying me drinks and asking what my name was and I was saying it was Beyoncé Esmeralda Biggentitten which obviously it isn't but at eighteen I can now LEGALLY CHANGE IT BY DEED POLL. And then Carrie says, ''Ere Shiraz, what's left on your list now?' So I looked at the list and said, 'OMG! I can legally get married without my mum's consent!!!' And Carrie screamed, 'OH MY GOD!! WHO WILL YOU MARRY???' and to be honest my mind went totally blank and then I thought about Wesley Barrington Bains II and his flat overlooking the pakora factory that he wants me to move into. But then the weirdest thing happened. I looked over at the bar and I couldn't believe my eyes because standing there, buying two gin and tonics, was DANNY JACOBS FROM WORKING MAGIC!!!!!!

DANNY JACOBS!!! Standing with another lad. Seven million people in London and I bump into him!!! It was FATE!!! And his mate was almost as bare choong as he was! And Danny looked so happy to see me! He gave me a hug and kissed me on both cheeks. And he stayed out with us in the bar in Camden for the next few hours and we were just chatting and laughing and he gave me his mobile number and he put mine in his phone but he never tried nothing on as I think he is a total gentleman.

Oh my life. Danny is so lush. And he's into ALL the same types of things as me too. He likes Beyoncé and Kylie and *EastEnders* and silly reality TV and he knows all about fashion and celebrity gossip and stuff like that!!

And he can't STAND football at all! And he's so well dressed and he looks after his skin. How good is that for a bloke eh?!! And his mate Christian was nice too. Saying that Carrie wasn't getting nowhere flirting with Christian, he weren't having none of it. And at some point I found out that Mint Lass won the 2.15 in Carlisle! And by this point I was thinking that this was probably the BEST BIRTHDAY IN THE WORLD EVER.

And I was so giddy by the end of it and there are big parts I don't even remember at all in fact the last bit I remember properly is shouting "Ere Carrie the one thing I've missed out is getting a tattoo!' And I don't really remember much else after that at all. And I really should get out of bed today and watch *EastEnders Omnibus* but I can't be arsed and for some reason my right ankle really really bloody hurts like I've burned it or something.

7pm – Oh god, no. NO NO NO NO NO

WEDNESDAY 7TH OCTOBER

I'm beginning to see the funny side of the tattoo now. It's only little. About as big as a penny. It's on my right ankle. It's a tiny little loveheart with 'Shiraz' written under it. 'You demanded it!!' Carrie keeps saying. 'Me and that Danny boy and his friend Christian tried to stop you! You shouted you were an adult and you would do whatever you bloody wanted!!!'

Oh crapping hell. I don't want to be an adult if it's like

totally my responsibility what happens to me. I liked it much better when I was sixteen and I could blame my mum or the teachers at Superchav Academy or the council or whatever.

But being a grown-up with my own flat means I'm in charge of all sorts of bloody boring stuff. Bills and council tax and working every bloody day. Like this week the hot water has totally stopped working and I've called Mr Drossos our Greek landlord ten times but he is TOTALLY BLANKING me.

So the last two days I've just squirted more *J-Lo Glow* on and washed my pits with water from the kettle. God I actually miss our bathroom in Goodmayes which had a lot of bumsmells but always had hot water. And Carrie leaves our bathroom in a right mess. She covers it in used knickers and cotton wool and Tampax inner tubes and balls of crumpled tissue with snot on them and OMG it's like she has never ever cleaned up after herself in her whole life ever!!! Carrie can't even remember to take the plug out of the bloody bath herself like she thinks I'm her maid or something.

Actually where is Carrie? I've not seen her for days?

THURSDAY 8TH OCTOBER

Still no hot water. Left six new messages on Mr Drossos's phone. And I still haven't learned any facts about London to tell to the tourists. There is only so many times

I can say 'Behold the magnificent panoramic view!' and wave my arms around for thirty minutes before it gets boring. And today someone asked me for a short history of Big Ben and I didn't have a bloody clue. So I made something up proper quick and said that Big Ben was the name of a real-life giant called Benjamin who owned the clock back in medieval times, in approximately 1066. I said that obviously Big Ben didn't look so big to him, what with him being a huge giant. In fact he used to call it Little Ben.

Well all the tourists were proper amazed at that. And then one annoying German bloke says, 'Excoooze me miss. I am preety sure zat Big Ben eez the name of zee actual bell inside zee clocktower at Westminster! And I think zee tower vas built in 1834!' So I just gave old Hanz Kneezanbumpsadaisy the evils and he shut his gob and thankfully no one told the supervisor Jayne Deacon or I would have WELL BEEN IN TROUBLE.

FRIDAY 9TH OCTOBER

Still no hot water!!! Agggghhh! Mr Drossos promised he'd send someone out too! I've got a good mind not to pay my part of the rent!! OK, I've got a good mind to tell Barney Draper not to cover my bit of the rent till I can pay him back. Carrie has been out all week with her new boyfriend Jimmy Di Marco. I don't know anything about him yet other than he is 'bare lush' and 'properly THE one' and she gave him a massage at Butterz and 'sparks flew'. She was off to a wine bar.

I'm skint so I stayed in and used her fancy cream to bleach my moustache.

SATURDAY 10TH OCTOBER

AAAAAAAGH! STILL NO HOT WATER!!

I am trying to look on the bright side. I think you can get quite a decent wash with just Boots antiseptic wet wipes. Far more hygienic than lying about in a bath in your own dirty water. Plus I am getting really really good at this London Eye thing. To be honest you can say whatever you like really and people believe you! In fact they like the lies even better! Danny from Working Magic was right, sometimes people don't want me to be so real.

Like yesterday, I told some American tourists that we still have prisoners like IRA bombers and animal rights extremists in the Tower of London dungeons. This ain't true at all. In fact I think that's where the gift shop and café is. But then I got a bit carried away and told them we had folk actually strrrrretched out screaming on medieval torture racks with proper long arms screaming for a pardon from Her Majesty the Queen. And then I said that every second Thursday of the month they sell tickets at Trafalgar Square and behead a paedophile! Well the Texans in my pod thought that was very interesting and gruesome! And one even gave me a tenner tip at the end!

Actually, that's quite bad isn't it? Right that's it. NO MORE LIES ABOUT LONDON.

SUNDAY 11TH OCTOBER

Today was my first day off in FOR EVER.

I'd arranged to see our Murphy weeks back but I never thought anything would come of it. 'Cos it's not like Murphy has a social diary to write stuff down in. And I sent him a text and said, I AM OFF WORK SUNDAY 11TH OCT, he just texted back saying TRU DAT INNIT. LATERZ. MURPHDOG. Even I didn't know what that bloody meant. So I was proper surprised this morning when he rang me up.

I arranged to meet Murphy outside Nike Town at Oxford Circus on Oxford Street at 1pm. And when I got there he was standing chatting on his mobile. He had a baseball cap on and a black jacket and extra baggy jeans with his boxers coming out of the back. Well tall he looked too! And sort of older. And more hairy, like Year Eleven boys start being.

And when I walked up to him I saw he had a bit of a lovebite on his neck! So I pointed at it straight away and he went pink and said, 'Ugh girl dem, sis' and pulled his hoodie hood up! And I felt well weird as I thought, 'God I never saw you getting so much older when I used to see you every day.' And I felt proper silly then as I had been planning on taking him to Hamleys Toy Shop on Regent Street first to look at all the soldiers and model aircraft.

That idea seemed well wack now.

So we walks down Regent Street and we're chatting about Goodmayes and I'm asking him for all the latest gossip. And thing is, I used to think our Murphy was well crap with gossip. Now I'm thinking that maybe me and Cava-Sue just never used to let him speak. 'Cos he's telling me about the Brunton-Fletcher family who are back in Thundersley Road in full effect being proper shady as ever. 'Man, hundred per cent to the max.' says Murph. 'But big up Uma, she ain't getting involved like or nuttin'. And like the whole clan are back now. Uma's mother Rose. Rose's babyfather. All the brats. They roll deep innit?' And I laughed a bit 'cos the Brunton-Fletchers do roll deep but it ain't so funny for Uma.

'Have you seen Uma around Mayflower Academy?' I asks him. 'Is she doing her A-levels?'

'Dunno man, ain't spotted her ever,' he says. Oh god. That made me feel well sad.

But then Murphy made me proper giggle talking about Cava-Sue and Mum. 'Oh Moonmask, you are well out of it! I ain't feeling it living there at the moment, know what I'm saying? It's like living in a warzone.' So I asks what they were arguing about and he says, ''Ow to bring up Cava-Sue's baby. And it ain't even popped out yet! Where's it gonna sleep? What's it gonna eat. What's it gonna be called. And last night Cava-Sue starts talking about feeding the baby? Y'know, with her boob! And Mum's going "'Ow long you gonna do that for, one month or something?" And our Cava-Sue goes "No, till the baby decides itself that it don't want it! And some babies do it until they're two years old!!"' Murphy's face was proper funny when he told me that. 'Man I thought I was gonna spew!' he says.

I didn't know where to take Murphy after that 'cos we were both pretty skint, but at least it was quite a nice day and the sun was out, so we kept on walking to Hyde Park and we got two 99 ice-creams with flakes and we just kept wandering, chatting, and I thought Murphy would start moaning but he never did. It was like he was just happy being away from Goodmayes.

He was telling me about school and how he's been thinking about specialising in IT and doing a college course next year, 'cos one of Tariq's brothers works in the city and he makes £50k a year! 'Don't tell Mum though,' Murphy says. 'You know what she's like. I never tell her stuff like that. She just puts you off.'

'I know,' I says. 'I'll keep it a secret.'

And somehow before I knew it, it was 6 o'clock, so we both had a Mcdonalds 'cos we were starving, then Murphy said he was off home. And we gets to Oxford Circus tube again and Murphy says, 'So are you back at work tomorrow then selling houses and that?'

So I thought for a bit then I says ''Ere Murphy, I'll let you into a secret too. I ain't an estate agent. I just said that 'cos somehow it stopped Mum doing my nut in.'

So Murphy looks at me and bursts out laughing and

says, 'No way! No way man! What do you do really?'

And I goes, 'Oh this and that. I'm OK though. Don't worry.'

Murphy laughs and says, 'Oh what are you like sis!? That is bare jokes. Too jokes man! Ha ha ha ha!'

I could still hear him laughing as he disappeared down the steps to the tube. Today was a pretty good day.

TUESDAY 13TH OCTOBER

TODAY WAS A VERY VERY BAD DAY. I have just been fired from the London Eye! Oh bloody crapping hell! The money was really good too! Oh I don't believe this. I can't believe I didn't suss out that one of those tourists would film me talking on his mobile phone and put me up on YouTube. Aaaaagh! And he uploaded me under the heading 'Funniest Tourguide Ever'.

Oh god! And it was that day last week that I was telling a group of tourists from Canada that St Paul's Cathedral was actually built by Saint Paul himself during Biblical times. And Paul made the main dome part of it all round with a point on the end like a big woman's boob to remind the menfolk of London about the sin of temptation.

Well, none of this is true at all. I was just freestyling, 'cos I'd worked out by this point that fake history is much more fun than real history. And whenever I told the people on the London Eye REAL history everyone just looked bloody bored and started asking me to take group photos of them again. Or take HILARIOUS photos of them pretending to push Big Ben over.

And by the way SPIN ON IT JAYNE DEACON I DON'T WANT YOUR BLOODY JOB. YOU CAN KEEP IT! I DON'T NEED YOU! I DON'T NEED YOUR DOLLAR!!!!!

THURSDAY 15TH OCTOBER

Oh god. I need another job soon. I need someone's dollar. Anyone's bloody dollar.

MONDAY 19TH OCTOBER

Danny called me today. He'd heard about the YouTube thing. 'How? Did Jayne Deacon call you?' I says and he goes, 'No Shiraz it's up on the YouTube home page as a "recommended video". It's had 626,876 views already.' And that's when I started crying and Danny said to calm down and he'd take me for lunch.

We met up in Soho which is the proper central part of London where it always feels like there's tonnes going on. Everyone seems really cool in Soho. That's where Carrie reckons loads of the media stuff goes on. I met Danny in this place called Bar Italia which is just near a place called Old Compton Steeet. We sat in the window watching loads of fit men go by. Then Danny says, 'Look, cheer up princess. It's not that bad.'

And I says, 'It IS that bad Danny! Look at all these people outside! They all have jobs! They manage to survive in London! They manage to do jobs! Me, I'm going to have to go home to Goodmayes and live in a house with my sister who's gonna breastfeed her kid until it's two and apparently plans to do it in Aldi if need be 'cos after all it's only nature!'

Well, Danny laughed and put his arm around me which felt lovely. 'Danny, how do people get amazing jobs like that Kitten Montague-Jones at *London Alive*?' I said. I'd just been reading her column Kitten's Titbits in *London Alive* while waiting for him to come. Danny just laughed and said, 'Oh god, 'cos her dad plays golf with the managing editor and her mum's having an affair with the chairman of the company. Probably. In fact definitely. Listen Shiraz, it's just different rules for people like them, they do whatever they want.' Then he rolls his eyes like a tiny girl would. He makes me laugh when he does that.

'OK, don't panic,' he says. 'Look, there are thousands of jobs out there. And at least we're beginning to identify your strengths and weaknesses. And . . . what we've worked out is that a) You need any job at the moment, ANYTHING and b) Preferably a job which doesn't involve you speaking that much to the general public and c) You want to feel like you're in London and not trapped in some cellar and d) Shiraz, you're not terribly good at taking orders. But that's FINE, we can work on that! We just need to find you something quick to earn you some food to feed you right now! Don't we?'

'Yes,' I said. 'That's right.' And then I wiped my eye make-up on a Bar Italia serviette and he squeezed my waist again which felt even better the second time.

'Right,' he says. 'OK, I think I might have a few ideas.' THANK GOD!!!! HE'S CALLING ME ABOUT IT TOMORROW!!!

THURSDAY 22ND OCTOBER

Oh my god. I wish I was dead.

FRIDAY 23RD OCTOBER

No. I still can't write about it.

SATURDAY 24TH OCTOBER

Today was so bad I actually wished one of those bendy buses on Regent Street would mount the pavement and kill me. Still, got paid today tho', so I can eat.

WEDNESDAY 28TH OCTOBER

I got up this morning at 8am and I tried the hot water again like an idiot and it still wasn't working and then I put on all my warmest clothes and a woolly hat and two jumpers and a scarf and then I got the tube into the West End and I collected my sign from the back of the shop where we keep them and then I went down to my spot outside the posh department store called Liberty and then I held up the massive enormous neon orange sign in the air telling everyone about the Golf Sale.

And most of the day people ignored me like I was invisible. And about once every hour some proper comedian who was with a big group of friends would walk up and say, 'Excuse me, do you know if there's a golf sale anywhere!!!!?' and then wet himself laughing and everyone laughed with him. And at 2pm it really really rained and I hid under a fire escape down a back lane and got scared stupid by a tramp lying in a pile of boxes who I thought was dead but was just sleeping. And I came home tonight and Carrie was out again so I was in the flat by myself again and I'm not sure how much else I can take.

THURSDAY 29TH OCTOBER

I got a splinter in my hand today from holding the Golf Sale sign. I am proper unhappy. I think Shiraz Bailey Wood has to have a serious think about her life.

FRIDAY 30TH OCTOBER

OK something properly good has happened tonight. I totally wasn't expecting it. To start feeling so different all of a sudden. So I was at work today and I get a lot of time to think at work so I starts thinking about my Wesley Barrington Bains II. I've been meaning to call him for ages. I was missing him a bit I suppose. Just the way he is always proper calm and kind, 'cos London isn't calm or kind at all.

So I called him and said hello and he sounded well happy to hear from me which was good 'cos I was worried he might be a bit weird.

So he asked if I'm all right and I said, 'No not really.' And I tell him about how we'd had no hot water for weeks and that I was feeling a bit down.

So he goes, 'Are you moving back to Goodmayes then, innit?'

And I goes, 'I don't know.'

And then he says, 'Look are you in your flat tonight, I'll give you a bell proper innit.' So I said I was.

So when I got home, first thing I see outside Paramount Mansions is a banana-yellow Golf. And then I see Wesley Barrington Bains II sitting on the doorstep with his tool box! He looks up and sees me and smiles. 'Why didn't you ring me about your boiler sooner, innit?' he says.

'Oh, I didn't want to bother you,' I said. But really I didn't want him to know how skint I was. Or that I'm not an estate agent. So Wesley comes inside and I put the kettle on and he smells of his usual Kouros aftershave and he's looking quite buff really, if I'm being honest. Well I can't believe what happened next.

So after about twenty minutes of hitting things with his spanner there's a big noise in the boiler cupboard!! And then the water came on!! And half an hour after that I had a lovely big hot bath! And Wesley stayed for his supper and we got some pizza delivered and we watched *I'm A Celebrity* and Wesley and me sat on the sofa and had a right laugh just like the old days.

And then Wesley says to me, 'Shiraz, I miss you loads like, innit.'

And I looks at him and says, 'Aw I miss you too Wesley.' And he leans forward well close to me and says, 'Look I think I've got to be proper straight up with you, innit.'

And I was kind of listening to him but the thing was my mobile phone was ringing. So I gets it out of my handbag and OMG it said DANNY JACOBS CALLING! Danny was calling me on a Friday night! So I picked it up and Danny was in this bar in Soho but he said he had some news.

Danny says that he has FOUND me the perfect job! And it's a job where I can use my 'theatrical' talents!! And it's a job which lasts right up to Christmas!!! Amazing eh? What a turnaround, eh? The hot water is fixed, Danny Jacobs called me on a Friday night which means he was thinking about me AND I'VE PROBABLY GOT AN AMAZING NEW BLOODY JOB.

Wesley left soon after that. I don't really know what happened. He got the hump all of a sudden and went. Boys are proper weird sometimes, aren't they?

NOVEMBER

MONDAY 2ND NOVEMBER

I LOVE House of Hardy on Oxford Street. I can't believe I work there. I mean, it's not like it's somewhere I'd ever go and actually buy something 'cos it is mad expensive, some of the designer sections on the top floors have handbags for like a grand and the assistants are well up their own bums, but I still really like going there 'cos it's so massive and from outside it looks proper old. And when I was a little girl one of the only times we ever got to come to London was to look at the House of Hardy Christmas window displays 'cos they do this thing where they decorate every single window with a Christmas scene. And sometimes they have moving mannequins and one time they even had a real live reindeer in the window eating carrots and doing poos! And they decorate the front of the store with like five billion fairy lights and best of all Santa Claus has a grotto on floor five and you can go and visit him! I don't know why it makes me all bumpy on my arms just thinking about it but it does.

Back in the day me and Cava-Sue and Mum used to come through on the train with Murphy in the push chair and sometimes it was snowing and dark and Oxford

Street was absolutely packed with people and we nearly used to lose each other and it was so exciting just the thought that at any minute I could get properly lost for ever. I still felt tingly like that today when I went for my training session. It was so weird 'cos this time I went in the special staff door in a back lane that I didn't know was there and went up to the offices on floor six.

I wasn't expecting that I would like Cindy Bushford, the House of Hardy supervisor, but she was proper nice. OK she was a bit bloody mental but still nice too. Cindy is an American and she is about forty and she has blonde wavy hair and sort of big eyes that don't blink much, as if someone has just told her a proper amazing secret and she is still totally flabbergasted.

So I sat in her office today and she looks at the forms Danny had sent over and she smiled and said, 'Well Shiraz, it says here that you have a very lively personality and a wonderful warm sense of humour and would be perfect as a member of our Christmas staff!'

'Mmm!' I said, not wanting to say anything that would stop her thinking that.

'And that's just wonderful because we just LOVE Christmas here at House of Hardy!'

'Mmmmmm!' I nodded.

'So I need to ask you a question, Shiraz,' says Cindy. 'Do you love Christmas too?' she says to me.

'Oh yes, I LOVE Christmas!' I said.

Now this was a bit of an exaggeration, I mean I *used* to

love Christmas, but it's not like I get those mental hyper buzzes about it like I did when I was seven and me and Murphy would get up at like 4am and eat selection box and then run round and round the tree until one of us sicked up Quality Street or something. But I do still like Christmas a lot. Christmas is proper special. But then Cindy suddenly says, 'And do you believe in Santa Claus, Shiraz?'

Well I didn't know what to say then 'cos she looked proper serious. Obviously, I knew she must be kidding, so just to be nice I kidded her back and said, 'Yes, of course I believe in Santa Claus! That's why I'm a nice girl all year round and not naughty, 'cos I want to be on his present list!'

Well, Cindy looked at me and then she looked proper relieved. Then she ticked a box on my form that said 'Accepted'. 'Excellent!' She smiled. 'That's a big relief. Shiraz Bailey Wood, welcome to the grotto!' Well I giggles a bit then 'cos I'm going to be one of Santa's little helpers! Or, to give you my official title 'Grotto Personnel: Elf Division' HA HA HA HA!

So then Cindy takes me up to the 'Elf training zone' to find me my outfit and she puts her hand on my shoulder and said, 'Oh you're going to just love SC! He is sooo adorable!'

'Who?' I says.

'Santa Claus,' she says. 'Unfortunately, he's resting today as he had a long trip from Lapland. He went via

Japan to check out some robotic dogs that are big this year. So he's a bit jet-lagged. But you'll meet him tomorrow, I hope.'

So I looks at her sort of funny, waiting for her to laugh and she doesn't, so I don't either. She just pulls that happy/surprised face again. And I really wanted to say, 'Cindy, you do know he's just an actor don't you?' but it didn't feel right.

'Anyway, let's meet the other elves!' she said, then started walking off proper fast down the corridor. This was one of the weirdest days of my entire life.

THURSDAY 5TH NOVEMBER

OMG – today was well hilarious. It was my first day of official elf duties. So I'm 'backstage' at House of Hardy and I'm in the locker room changing into my stripy tights and little green dress and my long blue hat with the bell and my long shoes with the curly point toes and I am nearly wetting myself laughing 'cos I look so funny. And I don't even feel embarrassed or nothing as I look so nothing like me that no one would even know it was me. And I'm having such a laugh with all the other elves, who aren't really elves of course, they're just other teenagers like me who need money. And they're from all over the world, like Petra is from Poland and Thor is from some weird place out in the sea past Scotland called the Outer Hebrides and Reuben is from South

Africa and Ritu is from Japan. So there's about thirty-five elves and we all work different shifts and the boys are pretty much all buff (when they're not wearing their curly shoes and false noses) and the girls are a really good laugh and believe me I owe Danny from Working Magic BIG TIME!!! I texted him this morning to say so and he texted back and said that he was on a last-minute break in Greece with his mate Christian in somewhere called Mykonos. He says the weather's not great this time of year but the bars are good. I hope he's not snogging too many girls.

So anyway, I didn't think there would be many grotto visitors today because, like WHO brings their kids to see Santa on the 5th November?? It's Bonfire Night, like, seven weeks away from Christmas. Well the answer is everyone in bloody London. We were mobbed! About two thousand children came! And the guy who plays Santa is proper amazing. He has a real big, fluffy white beard and twinkly brown eyes. He looks so real it is unbelievable. And he sounds just like Santa too. And he even laughs like Santa. And today I was walking to the store cupboard with Cassandra who is Cindy's assistant and I said, 'So where is Santa from really then? Is he from London?'

And Cassandra looked at me funny and says, 'SC is from Lapland. They have a log cabin out there, with a factory workshop attached where the gifts are wrapped and they have a room of computers to keep track of what child wants what. It's a pretty impressive organisation.'

And then Cassandra wandered off to find me the extra bags of glitter dust I needed to throw over the enchanted forest display. HA HA HA! I told you they were all a bit mental. Cassandra really looked like she thought Santa was real. Oh well. If they're going to pay me nine pound an hour plus a sandwich voucher then I'll believe in the Easter Bunny and the Tooth Fairy too. I'm all about keeping it real, but god am I sick of being skint.

11pm – He's not real though. Is he?

11.30pm – Oh bloody hell of course he's not. OMG I've only worked there one day!

FRIDAY 6TH NOVEMBER

OH MY DAYS – I don't know what is more tiring, the little kiddies who are so excited that you can't get them off Santa's knee, or the ones who wait proper patient and quiet for half an hour in the queue then catch sight of Santa and start to scream and scream and scream 'cos they're so frightened by his red cloak and crazy beard! Luckily almost everyone loves him. Actually, I love SC a bit too. He proper listens to all the kids. And he always knows what to say to them. Even the tiny, weeny ones who can hardly speak. And the ones who can't speak English. It's proper cute. I mean OK I know he's an actor and that . . . but sometimes when you're in the grotto and the lights are twinkling and he guesses exactly what a kid wants for

Xmas well . . . it's like he's not and . . . well, oh, it's a bit weird. And you can never catch Cindy or Cassandra out either, asking about him. And you never see him getting changed into being Santa. Or going home. Or arriving. It's like he . . . oh god Shiraz GET A GRIP he's not real!

It was so hard not to tell Cava-Sue about House of Hardy on the phone tonight – she still believes the story that I am 'selling luxury condos in Whitechapel'. To be honest though she wasn't really listening anyhow. Cava-Sue isn't very happy right now. Cava-Sue is thirty-seven weeks pregnant and says that she is so fat and ridiculous-looking that she can't even be bothered to stand up no more.

Cava-Sue says this baby is due in just over a week but doctors say it could come sooner or any time in like the next fortnight or even a bit more. Cava-Sue says if it's not next week she's going to sodding kill someone especially my mother. And then Cava-Sue says she feels like slapping that stupid nurse at the clinic who keeps saying her name wrong too. And then she said Lewis was annoying her too by 'keeping on asking her if she is OK all the time and making her cups of tea'.

And then Cava-Sue said that if she has to show her front-bits to one more complete stranger up at that pre-natal clinic she is going to go down Ilford X-change and sit on the counter at Magic Spuds and take her knickers off and shout, 'Oh come on then Essex, why don't you all have a look!?????' Then Cava-Sue said, 'Anyway Shiraz, keep your mobile switched on and I'll tell you when we have all systems go. You are coming aren't you Shiz? Don't worry, I'll get Lewis to blow up the paddling pool so you don't need to do that bit.' And then Cava-Sue had to go for another wee. In fact, she actually started weeing when I was on the phone as I could hear the trickle into the loo and her voice going all echoey in the bathroom.

As ever, Cava-Sue: TOO MUCH INFORMATION!

SATURDAY 7TH NOVEMBER

The grotto is getting even busier. Every time some kid chucks up with excitement in the enchanted garden I just try to remember the nine pound an hour and keep on spreading heavy elf-type good vibes. I owe Carrie like stacks of rent so I'm taking any shift I can. I'm having a good time though. It's nice having the other elves as mates now. Tonight me and Petra from Poland and Ritu from Japan went to Vue Cinema after work and then Ritu took us to a Japanese bar near Oxford Street and we had Japanese beer called Asahi and some noodles and Ritu tried to teach me how to use chopsticks! I am bloody rubbish. Ritu says it's 'cos I am being too dainty and English. Ha! Me? Dainty!? Ritu says get the bowl up near your mouth and just slurp the liquid and stuff the noodles in with the sticks and don't worry 'cos that's what Japanese people do. I did that and it was much better. I like London 'cos you learn stuff like that every day.

2am – Tonight I went out with Carrie and her new boyfriend Alfonso. Alfonso is one of Jimmy di Marco's friends. Well he *was* anyway. They don't speak no more 'cos they fell out over who was dating Carrie. 'Cos they both were. There was a bit of an 'overlap', she reckons. Carrie can be a hooch sometimes. In a nice way, of course. Anyway, Alfonso is a club promoter. I'm not sure what that means. He's something to do with this club called Obtuse in Belgravia in London. He puts this night on Sunday called 'Durrty'. So whenever you see Alfonso he's always on his mobile phone shouting about guestlists or bragging about money. And he's not even that buff or nothing – he looks like a young version of Mr Yolk who runs the café in Goodmayes but he's got a Porsche 911 so Carrie thinks he is bare choong.

So anyway, I went to Durrty tonight with Carrie but we didn't go out till about midnight 'cos Carrie spent three hours straightening her hair 'cos she said all sorts of celebrities and footballers would be in there. And we were on Alfonso's list for the VIP room so we had to look superbuff. Carrie was celebrating getting a high C in her Butterz Beauty Academy mid-term exam. Personally, I think what she really needs to celebrate is not getting slung out on her arse. She's had two warning letters to the flat already about her bad attendance. It's just like Superchav Sixth Form again. Poor Barney Draper, this beauty school thing is costing him a bomb.

I felt proper nervous about going to Durrty at Obtuse 'cos it is totally the sort of club that you see in *Heat* magazine with all them celebs staggering out of the door drunk and members of the Royal Family head-butting paparazzi and that. I couldn't imagine me in there really and I worried about money but Carrie said don't be daft then she lent me one of her Gharani Stok frocks and said it's not like we'll be paying for any drinks 'cos we know Alfonso.

Tonight was sort of good I suppose. The music was OK. R&B and Hip Hop and all that. And I saw that Angel Jackson girl from *Big Brother* dancing on a table and then chucking up in a plantpot. And I saw that Kitten Montague-Jones too down there with her mates being all rowdy and asking where the Very VIP part of the VIP area was 'cos they wanted to stand in there instead, 'away from the riffraff'. Well Alfonso didn't really have a Very VIP room, so he sort of invented one for them and let them stand in the room where the cleaners keep their mops and stuff. Well Kitten was much happier then and she bought more champagne. I can't understand how she writes all these columns for papers and that. I reckon she's a bit backwards.

So it was sort of funny. But I find it all a bit weird really. I can't work out how people afford to go out clubbing on a Sunday night in places like Durrty. A bottle of champagne costs three hundred pound!!! And they sell them all night long. And sometimes people just buy them and spray them on the floor. And I totally felt like the only person in there who was getting up in four hours to go to work. Carrie said I shouldn't tell anyone about the Christmas grotto job as it wasn't exactly cool so I didn't mention it. But then I didn't have anything else to talk to anyone about so I didn't say much at all.

I dunno why, but tonight when everyone was dancing and throwing wine about I kept thinking about this woman called Kimberlee who is a cleaner at House of Hardy. She's from Rwanda. She cleans every night in the store from 3am until 8am. I sometimes see her and we have a chat. Kimberlee came to London in a proper hurry a few years back 'cos there was this big fight in her village and loads of the men from one tribe killed loads of men from another tribe with axes. I'm not supposed to know about the axes bit. Kimberlee never says anything about it but Ritu told me 'cos she studied African History at University and she said it was proper awful.

Anyway, so I comes into work this morning far too early 'cos I set the clock on my phone fast by accident and I'm by myself pulling on my costume in the locker room when all of a sudden I hear this weird sound. Like a snoring sound. And it was coming from a locker. One of those really big lockers that you can almost put a suitcase in if need be. It sounded like our dog Penny snoring after a big dinner. And I felt really scared. But then I went towards the locker and gently opened the door and inside, I couldn't bloody believe it, there was a tiny little girl!!! About two years old! In a nightie with a blanket wrapped around her and a dummy in her mouth. And she didn't even wake up. I couldn't believe what I was seeing! So I shut the door. Then I turned around and ran proper fast and ran straight into one of the other cleaners coming the other way and she saw my face all red and she grabbed my arms and said, 'What the matter girl, you OK?' So I said, 'Little girl! Little girl!' and the cleaner grabbed me with both hands and whispered and said, 'Shhhhhhh! It is Kimberlee's little girl. Kimberlee need to earn money. She has no one to look after her girl. So she need to bring her sometime. But shsssshhh no tell Cindy. It a big secret. Please.'

So I promised I wouldn't tell no one. No one at all. So, anyway, I suppose that's what I was thinking about tonight at Durrty when I was watching Kitten Montague-Jones pouring three hundred pound champagne over her head. I was thinking that if Kimberlee at work had that three hundred pound she could pay a baby-sitter then her little girl wouldn't have to sleep in that smelly House of Hardy locker and OH MY LIFE! I AM STARTING TO GO ALL POLITICAL LIKE BLOODY CAVA-SUE! Well, like Cava-Sue before she got pregnant and just started harping on about her inverted nipples and pelvic floor all the time.

Ha ha ha! Oh my days. Cheer up Shiraz you silly cow!!!!

WEDNESDAY 18TH NOVEMBER

PROPER FUNNY DAY. So I'm in the grotto and to be honest I'm in a bit of a dark mood 'cos some brat had just took a mentaloid fit in the enchanted forest and knocked down about four trees, and this other woman had decided to change her baby's nappy behind Santa's sleigh and leave the crappy nappy bunged behind one of the presents, but somehow I was still smiling 'cos there's something about being dressed as an elf that forces you to smile. Even if it's not a real smile. You can't be grumpy when you're an elf. A grumpy elf is just basically a goblin and a goblin ain't the same thing at all.

So I'm escorting a couple of Italian kids into Santa's little glade when Cindy appears and says she needs a chat. So I went to the office and she tells me not to worry 'cos I must have looked proper worried and then she says that they have been 'conducting a customer services survey amongst grotto-goers' and that I had been named EIGHTY-SEVEN times as 'Best Elf'!!! And that meant I'm 'Employee of the Fortnight!' Well I was really smiling then! So then she says, 'Now SC has been informed and he has a special House of Hardy gift certificate for fifty pounds to present to you. Please go in and see him at the end of your shift.'

'OK,' I said, giggling again.

So it gets to 6pm and I'm kind of wishing they'd just give me the bloody voucher 'cos I'm knackered and I'm sure the bloke who plays SC is too, then Cassandra says, 'Shiraz, SC can see you now.' So I goes into the little room where he sits and there's SC sitting on his chair, looking all twinkly and lovely with his glasses on the end of his nose and he's eating a mince pie and drinking a cup of tea out of his special white china cup on a saucer. He's got crumbs all down his fluffy beard and red jacket. And he sees me and says, 'Shiraz Bailey Wood, come in, come in. Welcome, Elf of the Fortnight!'

So I laughs and says, 'OK Santa, it's OK – I know you're off duty now.' 'Cos I wanted to remind him that I was bloody eighteen and knew he was an actor.

But he just ignored that and passes me the envelope with the voucher and says, 'Thank you for all your hard work, Shiraz! My grotto couldn't function without elves like you!'

So I laughs and takes the voucher but I was feeling sort of weird now as he was still being one hundred per cent Santa and he was proper convincing. 'And what would you like for Christmas, Shiraz?' says SC.

'Ooooh, erm, dunno really,' I says, smiling at him. 'I wouldn't mind an iPod shuffle,' I said.

'Oh yes, yes, iPods are always popular,' SC says. 'So would an iPod bring you happiness?' he says.

So I thought for a bit and said, 'Errrrrrm, dunno. I think just the hard cash instead would make me happy really. London is proper expensive.'

Then SC laughs proper loud and says, 'Yes, very true,

although not as expensive as Stockholm. The accountant at my Head Office in Lapland has terrible trouble keeping to their Swedish budgets! Toys are very very pricey indeed.' Well I expected him to wink or something then. But he didn't, he just sipped his tea and smiled in his jolly Santa way. This was all a bit mental. Then SC goes, 'So what does the New Year hold in store, Miss Wood? Do you have a Christmas wish for that?'

Well that sort of stumped me. 'Oh my days,' I says. 'I ain't got a clue, SC. It's all about living in the moment right now for Shiraz Bailey Wood. Get me?'

'I get you,' says SC.

Now this is totally true. I still don't know what to do with my life. I mean, I jacked in Mayflower Sixth Form to go off and have an adventure. But I'm starting to think that to have a proper adventure in life maybe I really needed to finish school first. And all the jobs I'd like to do, well I've no idea how you get them and no one else can tell me either, other than 'It helps if your godfather is the managing director'. It's well confusing.

'So you'll be an elf again next Christmas?' SC says. Well I started giggling now 'cos I knew he was trying to trick me into saying, 'Oh bloody hell no! Hopefully I'll be doing something a bit better!' But I didn't, I said, 'Well, hopefully by next year I'll be doing something more like I really want to do. Y'know, in media? Or something creative. 'Cos, y'know, I like being creative. I like to write stuff down and I like to make up little stories and words and make people laugh and things. I'd like to do something where I can do that. That's what my wish is really,' I says. It felt weird saying it loud 'cos I never really say it out loud, but this was SC, after all.

So SC nods his head and says, 'OK then, well I'll do my best. I'm sure a clever girl like you will go very far.' Then he laughs his funny ho ho ho laugh and I giggles and then he shakes my hand with his big warm hand and then I went home on the tube holding my fifty quid voucher feeling well tripped out like someone had spiked my lunchtime sandwich with magic mushrooms.

I hope House of Hardy pay SC loads of money 'cos he is the best Santa ever.

FRIDAY 20TH NOVEMBER

9.30pm – Whitechapel

Cava-Sue reckons her baby is coming. She says her contractions have begun. I'm getting the last train back to Goodmayes now. I'm well nervous and it's not even me pushing the thing out of me. Oh my days I am frightened.

SUNDAY 22ND NOVEMBER

10pm – Whitechapel.
******THIS HAS PROBABLY BEEN THE MADDEST WEEKEND EVER******

So I got home to Thundersley Road about midnight on Friday night. I imagined I'd get home and find Cava-Sue arguing and being all lairy but when I got to Thundersley Road she was actually quite chilled out. Well actually more than chilled. She's sitting in the kitchen at the little table being proper quiet. And her belly's enormous like that big fat Buddha that Spirit of Siam Chinese Takeaway have got in their window, but the rest of her seemed proper small and scared. And she weren't shouting or giving anyone orders. She was just sat there in her black Theatre of Dead T-shirt and a pair of Lewis's trackie bottoms with her hair all greasy up in a scrunchie. She looked on a different planet to be honest. It was like she'd sort of given up on life and decided to let it do whatever the hell it bloody wanted. I weren't expecting that at all. This made me feel more scared 'cos Cava-Sue is my big sister and she always usually knows what to do.

Mum and Lewis and our dog Penny were there too. Dad and Murphy were both in their beds 'having an early night'. For some daft reason my throat went all crackly when I saw my sister and I gave her a kiss and made us both a cup of hot Ribena 'cos that was all she fancied. Then I put Radio One on the kitchen radio and I did her my stupid Tim Westwood impression which always makes her smile. She cheered up a bit then. Then I told her a load of my really bad jokes about ducks walking into chemists and sandwiches walking into pubs and eventually she started laughing and said, 'Oh shut up,

Shiraz you donut.' So then I got out *Heat* magazine and made her look at celebrities picking their knickers out of their bum crevices or with bogies hanging out of their noses and we gossiped about girls we went to school with who Cava-Sue's met down pre-natal classes and the idiot blokes they've got themselves preggo by.

And every so often Cava-Sue would go, 'Oh bloody hell, here it comes, it's like sodding turbo bloody charged period pain or something.' Then her face would go all scrunched and upset. But then after a few minutes it would pass again. And sometimes she'd stand up and just grip on to the side of the fridge and swear. But Mum never said nothing about the swearing. Mum would just come in and rub the bottom of Cava-Sue's back and nag Lewis to ring the midwife again to find EXACTLY when she was coming or start nagging Cava-Sue to change her mind about this home birth and go to the hospital.

But Cava-Sue wasn't having none of that. And Cava-Sue didn't want the bloody paddling pool now either, thank you very much, she just wanted to have the baby on the floor and I thought Mother would start doing her nut about her new rug from the catalogue but she didn't. And then a really, really big contraction came and Cava-Sue just leaned against the fridge then actually pushed herself down on to the floor and sat there for a bit sweating, shouting, 'Oh my god! I hate this! I can't bloody do this. What am I doing!? I can't do this!' Then Lewis sat down beside her in amongst Penny's dog dishes and said, 'Oh come on Cav, you're well clever you are! You can do this. I know you can. The baby's going to be here soon. Our baby! We're gonna have a baby Cava-Sue!' And Cava-Sue shouts, 'I bloody know that Lewis I'm the one lying here like a bloody stoned tellytubby!!' And then we all laughed.

And then Cava-Sue started making a really weird sound. Not like moaning. More like a cow mooing. And Lewis was holding her hand they were telling each other how much they loved each other and Lewis started crying and they were talking about the time they went to Vietnam and wittering on about weird temples they had visited and total nonsense like that. And at 2am the midwives arrived THANK BLOODY GOD and started sticking their hands in places and measuring Cava-Sue's bits and shouting out orders and made Cava-Sue move into the living room and lie on the floor on a pile of towels with her legs apart.

Well my plan was that I wasn't watching any of the gory stuff. I thought it was going to be like when people have babies on *EastEnders* and it lasts like about seven minutes. And I could just stay up at the top end and shout 'PUSH'. But it wasn't like that at all. It lasted for another five hours. FIVE HOURS. Five hours of mooing and swearing and pushing! And when the head started arriving I couldn't help but go and look. It was the most amazing disgusting brilliant thing I have ever seen in my life and ever will again I reckon. A little tiny human head. With hair! Lots of brown hair! I thought babies were bald? AND OH MY GOD it was totally horrible to watch but I couldn't stop looking 'cos it was so weird. Our mum couldn't stand it so she went out and sat on our doorstep and when I looked out to check I'm sure she was praying 'cos she had her face in her hands talking to someone so it had to be God, 'cos even I'd gone to the loo and had a pray and I never do normally, but I wanted God to help us, 'cos this was so bloody scary.

Well, right near the end it got really really bad, 'cos Cava-Sue was so tired she couldn't push any more and the midwives were going, 'Just one more time! Come on! Start breathing then push! PUSH!' And Cava-Sue let the loudest moo out ever and I still have no idea even now how the next bit happened because Cava-Sue is small and the thing she was pushing out was HUGE but then suddenly WOOOOOOOOOSH! The baby just sort of slid out! And the midwives grabbed it and rubbed it and Lewis was crying and I was crying and Cava-Sue was sort of squeaking and one of the midwives who was this really clever looking African woman said, 'This baby seems in good shape. Cava-Sue you've got a little boy!'

IT'S A BOY! I'VE GOT A NEW NEPHEW! He was all squawking and covered in goo but beautiful anyway and then Mum came running in and just burst into tears too. Then they let Cava-Sue hold him. And Cava-Sue looked proper esctatic but away with the fairies to be honest. And Lewis looked totally white and shocked and crumpled like he'd just been hit by a car.

My new nephew is bloody gorgeous. His face is a bit squashed and he's got lots of brown hair and he's quite red but the midwife says that'll sort itself out and he'll look more like a baby and less like a little monster soon! He is eight pounds and nine ounces! He's a whopper! His name is Epiphany Blaze Wood-Coombs. They're going to call him 'Fin' for short. Cava-Sue saw the word Epiphany in a travel book and she liked it 'cos it means 'A breakthrough of profound awareness'. We love a mental name do us Woods.

I've come back to Whitechapel now as it was well hectic at Thundersley Road and they needed the space. It's quite good to be back in my little bedroom in Whitechapel. My bedroom in Goodmayes doesn't really feel like mine now 'cos it's full of all of Fin's blankets and baskets and stuff. They call it Fin's room now, not Shiraz's. But I don't really mind at all.

Time moves on proper fast and you can't do nothing to stop it.

DECEMBER

WEDNESDAY 2ND DECEMBER

Oh my days we're going Christmas krrrrazy down at House of Hardy. Oh yes indeedydoody we are! We LOVE it! Hey, I tell you what track I sometimes like to play when I get home after a long shift? That Mariah Carey one, *All I Want For Christmas.* Cos I only hear it ONE HUNDRED AND EIGHTY-BLOODY-NINE TIMES a day while standing in a big crowd of squealing, farting, crying children, some of them so over-excited about meeting SC that they've actually taken leave of their bladders and weed into their pants and all over the floor. And one kid today decided he weren't bothering with the long queue so he came up and said he had cancer. AND HE DIDN'T. He just had eczema. And at one point we ran out of Santa's giftpacks and I thought a riot would break out because Mums and Dads were proper ripping them out of each other's hands and one dad offered another Dad an actual fist fight outside by the bins at 5pm. 'I'll take you down, mate! You've mugged yourself right off big time!' he was shouting as security wrestled him away through the enchanted forest.

I would also like to give special thanks to McDonalds who are giving away a free whistle, drum or kazoo with every Yuletide Happy Meal right now, so the kids are proper tooled up when they arrive to make some serious noise. I felt sorry for Thor from the Outer Hebrides today 'cos he'd been at his mate's birthday yesterday night and had a right old headache to start with. Well he eventually snapped at about 2pm and shouted at a kid from Cornwall with only one good eye who couldn't really walk proper for stepping all over his bloody curly slippers. 'WHAT ARE YOU, BLIND!!??' he yelled. Well it turns out the kid sort of was.

Cindy was quite chilled about it really. She didn't look that angry. But then we've worked out that Cindy has had loads of that Botox anti-age stuff injected in her face so it's pretty hard to know when she's got the hump. She has to walk right up to you and put her face proper close to yours and say 'I am NOT very happy' and even then you think she's joking 'cos her face looks sort of shocked/happy as if she was just sticking her trousers in the wash and found a lost tenner in the pocket. So anyway, the mood's sort of anxious in the grotto right now. If it weren't for SC and his good vibes we'd have all gone mad by now.

I came home tonight and wanted to have a moan about it all to Carrie but she weren't in again. She'd gone to one of her launches. She hardly invites me any more. I could tell she'd been home after Butterz and got changed and gone out 'cos she leaves a trail of evidence that you don't exactly need to be those dudes on *CSI* to work out. The door wasn't double locked. The stereo was still on. Her make-up was everywhere. There was shoes and tights and dresses everywhere. I tried tidying up but I was too knackered so I just cleared a big space in the middle of the sofa and ate my Cheese Strings and Mars Bar on my own. I'm not lonely. I don't mind being on my own. I like my own company. Honest.

SATURDAY 5TH DECEMBER

WE HAVE A NEW ARRIVAL! Ha ha ha!

So I was getting changed out of my elf outfit at about 6.30pm tonight when I gets this text from Carrie that says COME HOME QUICK WE HAVE AN EMERGENCY!!! so I call and Carrie whispers, 'Can't speak – not alone – need help NOW.' So I rush home thinking she's being raped and pillaged by a gang of crack-addled Mutant Ninja Turtles, but she ain't. I open the door and I can hear chatting. Carrie's clearly got company. And then a dog starts barking! And I can't believe who I see when I walk into the living room. Sitting on the sofa. UMA BRUNTON-FLETCHER AND ZEUS!!!! Uma's wearing a black padded jacket, skin tight navy jeans and trainers, looking a bit skinnier than normal and quite tired.

And Zeus spots me and runs over and puts both paws up on my shoulders and starts licking my face! 'All right Shiz!' Uma says to me, looking happy to see me.

'Bloody hell, Uma!' I said. And I was proper happy to

see Uma 'cos to be honest I've missed her. I looked for her last November when I was back in Goodmayes but her little sister told me she was in Portsmouth seeing her dad. Well, so they all guessed. None of the Brunton-Fletchers knew a hundred per cent where Uma was and that made me sad. So I rang Uma's pay-as-you-go and this right nutjob called Cuzzy picked it up and said this was his phone now 'cos he'd swapped it with Clinton for a debt. And the trail went cold after that.

So I sits down beside Uma and I can tell she's been crying. Now this is a pretty weird thing for me to see 'cos Uma Brunton-Fletcher never cries. NOT EVER. Uma is fierce. I mean, once in Year Nine I saw Latoya Bell slam Uma's hand in a door in the Science block 'cos Uma said she was a slut and Uma didn't even cry or nothing, she just walked over with the slammed hand that was proper red and throbbing and punched Latoya Bell smack central in the gob with it. That is how hard Uma Brunton-Fletcher is.

Anyway, Uma sat on the sofa and she told us her story. Uma says she went to Portsmouth for a bit 'cos Thundersley Road was getting too heavy now that Rose and Clinton and everyone came back and started selling weed and a bit of cocaine again. But when she got to Portsmouth her dad wasn't there – he was in prison for twenty-four days for non-payment of his drunk-driving fines. So she stayed with her sort of stepmum Mica, but Mica has a 'friend' staying there called Ricardo and

Ricardo was a bit of a pervert who kept asking to take pictures of Uma, so Uma pretended to go to the shop one morning and never went back.

So Uma went back to Thundersley Road but she didn't have a bedroom now 'cos her stepdad's kid Franklyn was in it. So Uma tried to crash down in the twins' bedroom instead but she didn't have a bed. But then last night, the police raided their house 'cos Clinton had a kilo of cocaine behind the fridge and they smashed all the doors off and ripped up the floorboards and smashed some windows too. So now Clinton is on remand awaiting trial and could get eight years but the house is wrecked and she just can't live there no more and she's well behind with A-levels to the point where she's practically dropped out. And then Uma started crying and I grabbed her hand and Carrie went and put the kettle on to make us some tea.

Then Carrie made Uma a sandwich and ran her a big bubble bath and Uma wandered off into the bathroom and I could hear her sitting on the loo still crying a little bit but softly. So Carrie looks at me and makes the shape with her mouth saying, 'She is NOT living here, Shiraz!' So I shuts the door and whispers, 'Where do you think she's gonna go then?' And Carrie whispers, 'It ain't our problem Shiraz!' Well this made me proper mad 'cos Uma, whatever has happened in the past, *is* our problem. She's our friend. She's been our friend for years. What about that time when she saved our bloody skins and organised that whole Prince Charles visit at Mayflower? What about when me and Carrie fell out in Year Ten and Bezzie dumped Carrie and Uma was a good friend to her? What about when I've been totally skint and Uma's had an on-line poker win and she's quite happily lent me twenty quid till I got paid? What about when that nasty rudegirl Jodeci from Chadwell Heath who didn't like Carrie started leaving nasty comments on Carrie's Bebo site saying she was a whore and she was going to beat her up? Within two days Uma managed to get Jodeci's pay-as-you-go number, call her and calmly inform her that if she made one more threat to Carrie then Uma would deal with it. And oddly enough Jodeci STOPPED threatening Carrie after that. And I know Uma can be a bit wild and her family are mentalists, but all in all, she is a good person. So what were we going to do, Carrie? Chuck her out on the street? It was *our* problem too! So I says this to Carrie and I says to her that she needs to sort her bloody head out 'cos if she thinks Alfonso and those airheads down at Durrty were her mates now well she's proper misguided and she needs to check herself and Carrie sort of rolled her eyes like she knew but she didn't want to hear it and then she called Alfonso and said she'd be late for dinner then she said, 'One week, Shiraz! They can both stay one week until Uma sorts her crap out. Then that's that.'

So I told Uma she could stay for a bit. We slept in my bed top to tail like you did at sleepovers when you were a kid. And at one point Zeus got in with us too 'cos he was lonely and cold. Two girls and a 110-pound Staffy all in one small bed fighting over the duvet. It was the funniest night ever. We sat up and gossiped till 5am. I'm glad Uma's staying for a bit. She's OK, she is.

MONDAY 7TH DECEMBER

Cava-Sue and Lewis sent me a little video on my phone today of Fin. He's got even bigger! And all his original brown hair is dropping out so he's sort of half bald with long strands of hair at the side that whisp over! And he's got a proper angry face too. Fin, if you ever find this diary in an attic in twenty years' time I want you to know that Aunty Shiraz always loved you but, mate, right now you wouldn't win no *Ilford Bugle* Bonny Baby competitions. You look like an angry slug.

I sent our Cava-Sue a text back saying that Fin's face was 'proper full of personality'. I didn't say it was the personality of someone who might get arrested down Romford Jumping Jaks for glassing people. Oh my days, I'm going to hell for thinking that! In other news Uma has made an appointment tomorrow to see Danny from Working Magic! It's my day off so I'm going to go with her.

WEDNESDAY 9TH DECEMBER

Yesterday really made me think about my life. About my attitude to it and how maybe I need to change it. So I got up at about nine and Carrie hadn't been home last night and Uma was already up, dressed and looking very smart in black trousers and a black fitted T-shirt with a slight V-neck. She's blowdried her hair straight and put on quite neutral make-up with strong dark lips and she looks sort of older. Uma's cleaned the kitchen and sterilised the work surfaces. She's tidied up the living room, emptied the bin in the bathroom and washed all the dishes and been down Somerfield and got bread, milk, eggs, cheese, potatoes, butter, soup, salt, tomato ketchup, teabags, two tins of tuna and some Winalot for Zeus. Uma didn't even seem to notice she'd been sorting things out. Like she'd done it in her sleep or something. I'd forgotten what the Brunton-Fletcher house was like when she lived there alone. It was her little kingdom. Proper clean. Always with a fresh tea-towel hanging over the oven door which used to make me laugh 'cos Uma ain't exactly Nigella bloody Lawson. I sat down on the sofa thinking 'Blooody hell, 10a Paramount Mansions has never felt so much like someone's home and not just Mr Drossos's flat that we live in.'

Uma made us poached eggs on toast. Then she asked about me and Wesley Barrington Bains II so I told her that we were over and Uma says, 'For ever?' and I says,

'Mmm yeah, I think.' And then Uma says that she saw my Wesley and his mate Bezzie Kelleher out down Life in Romford a few weeks back surrounded by girls so I stopped Uma talking about that 'cos I don't really like hearing about Wesley out without me. I don't know why. I wish that crap my mother said about first love being deepest would stop ringing in my bloody ears sometimes too.

So Uma asks me about my grotto job and I was making her laugh telling her stories about all the kids weeing and farting and vomiting then she says, 'You crack me up Shiraz. You've got this funny way of putting things you have. Hey didn't you want to be a writer or a journalist or something? You once told me that in English AS class. You're good at English aren't you?' So I says, 'Oh yeah, suppose I do, but that's never gonna happen.' Then I told Uma how impossible it was to get jobs like that. 'Oh what a load of old crap, someone's got to do it,' says Uma, lighting up an Embassy Red and sticking her head out of the window to blow the smoke. 'So why not you?' I didn't know what to say to her.

So then we went down Working Magic and my gorgeous sexy beautiful Danny was totally running late on his appointments so Uma had to see Angeliqua instead. Now this wasn't good news. Uma filled out her forms and Angeliqua looked at them and said, 'So you're interested in working in a casino, Miss Brunton-Fletcher? Have you got any formal training as a croupier?'

So Uma says no but she has worked unofficially as a croupier in Essex before. This is true 'cos her uncles used to run illegal gambling dens but she doesn't tell Angeliqua that. Then she explains that she's an expert in Five Card Poker, Stud Poker and Texas Hold 'em. She can also play Baccarat and Caribbean Stud and even Hong-Kong Mah Jong.

Well Angeliqua doesn't listen much to that and just starts moaning on about Uma 'requiring formal experience and Government Gaming Certificate 3129Q'.

But Uma just says, 'But surely if you help me find work in a casino then I can get some formal experience and the casino can help me apply for the certificate can't they? I've heard that's a way in?'

So Angeliqua just sighs and says she is sorry but it's the rules that she can't place her in a croupier job until she's had formal experience already. Well to me this sounded like a brick wall. But Uma says, 'OK, fine, well have you got any other jobs based in a casino then?' Then Angeliqua prints off a load of jobs cleaning loos and working in the kitchens in some of the flashier casinos in the West End. So Uma takes the print-out and says she's off to the café next door to have a look and she'll come back. And she thanks Angeliqua really politely for all her help, which I can't quite believe 'cos Angeliqua was being a right old cow.

So me and Uma sit down in a café and order teas and Uma looks down the list of cleaning jobs and gets out a pen and makes some notes. So then she rings the first one, the Imperial Palace, and asks to speak to the 'Human Resources Manager'. Then Uma tells the woman there that she's an experienced croupier just in the area with an A grade in certificate 3129Q and she's looking for work! I couldn't believe what I was hearing!

Well the manager at the Imperial Palace says they don't have any jobs and they usually recruit through Working Magic Agency anyhow, so Uma is even more pushy and says well could she pop in the casino with her CV as she's just stood outside? This was a lie. We were a mile away. So the woman says, 'Oh OK, go on then. Pass your CV to Mr Deng the duty manager. He's on the casino floor now.' So Uma puts down the phone, gets out her *A-Z*, finds the Imperial Palace, redoes her lipstick, changes out of her high-heeled shoes and into some pumps she had in her handbag and we run as fast as we can to the casino which is right down Tottenham Court Road, right down Oxford Street and then down a back lane in Dean Street.

And as Uma runs ahead I'm shouting, 'Uma! You don't have a CV to give him! Uma, you ain't an officially trained croupier!' But Uma just shakes her head and says, 'Don't stress about that now, Shiraz!' Then she buzzes the door, changes back into her high heels and we both go inside, Uma pulls her shoulders back and looks all tall and like she's supposed to be there and walks straight up to this oldish Chinese man sitting by the bar talking into his mobile phone and says, 'Mr Deng? I'm Uma Brunton-Fletcher. Working Magic Agency just sent me about the croupier job that is going?'

Well Mr Deng looked at her funny and said, 'How they know about that? I only fired him half an hour ago! Nothing keep secret in this casino!' So Uma gives him a huge smile like she's almost about to burst and I went and sat down at the side in the shadows of the closed casino and couldn't really believe what I was watching. First Uma explained to Mr Deng that unfortunately she'd just given her last CV to the Mandarin Garden Casino in Knightsbridge, but she'd email it over later to show how perfect she is for the job. And before I knew it Uma had talked Mr Deng and another croupier into playing poker with her to prove she knew all the jargon. Then she escorted him over to the Mah Jong tables and pushed the tiles around a bit and showed him she could play that too. Then she showed Mr Deng her card dealing skills. And then she even did a few card tricks for him like bloody David Blaine! And I sat there waiting for the moment when we got slung out of the place or disembowelled by Triad gangsters but it didn't happen.

And in the end Mr Deng admitted that he was stuck for a croupier tonight so she had to bring all of her paperwork then, but she could try out from 7pm to midnight because it's very rare that you 'get pretty English who play Mah Jong or Caribbean Stud like that.'

And Uma smiled and shook his hand and then we left. I honestly couldn't believe it. I felt dizzy as we walked down the stairs back out into the daylight. But Uma didn't look that shocked at all. She just lit up an Embassy Red and said, 'Well they had a job going didn't they? Somebody had to do it. May as well be me.'

At school they used to say that Uma had a bad attitude. What a load of crap.

SATURDAY 12TH DECEMBER

Uma took me out to the bars in Shoreditch tonight with her tips from Imperial Palace Casino. Uma is UNBELIEVABLE. She blagged her way through her Wednesday, Thursday and Friday night shifts without her paperwork but then she sussed that the Human Resources Manager was getting edgy about the paperwork, so she made sure Mr Deng had got a few double whiskies down his neck then took him aside and confessed that she'd not passed her gaming certificate at all. And Mr Deng said, 'Uma? What you do?! You get me in big trouble!' So Uma said she was REALLY, REALLY sorry but to work in the Imperial Palace Casino had been her big dream FOR EVER. This was a fib, she'd never heard of the place before Wednesday. But then Mr Deng was all flattered and he agreed to let her work there while she applied for the correct paperwork and they'd act as her 'named sponsor'. 'It good job all customers like you!

They say you funny girl and take no crap off no one!' Mr Deng said to her.

Uma might be a bit wild but she is proper clever and determined, deep down. She knew what she wanted and she went for it and she didn't take no for an answer. I need to be more like that.

I had good fun tonight. Me and Uma got dressed up, went out and went for beers in this boozer called the Old Blue Last. Then we walked home and got kebabs and an extra salami sausage for Zeus. The streets were full of drunk office-workers coming home from Christmas parties and people in Santa hats and people being sick out of taxis with tinsel in their hair. I don't feel so lost or scared walking about in London now. It's starting to feel like home.

MONDAY 14TH DECEMBER

Oh my days. I REALLY need to find a new job. SC is off back to Lapland in under two weeks and being realistic there ain't much need for happy elves in January. I looked at every single advert in the job section of *London Alive* today hoping for one what said 'Wanted – Totally unique individual for fabulous media job' or 'Untrained journalist needed to write stuff' or even 'TV presenter with no experience or skills needed to become famous!' but there wasn't. Everything sounded dead serious and needed two years' experience and a degree.

Uma says that I should get my ass back down that agency and get Danny to work his magic again. I says to Uma I know but I found it difficult talking about jobs with him 'cos the sexual chemistry between us was a bit overpowering. When Uma heard that she started laughing.

'Who? Danny who texts you right through *Coronation Street* some nights, making bitchy comments about the barmaid's outfits!?' she says.

And I says, 'Yeah!'

And Uma laughs again and says, 'What, Danny? The proper muscly one with the good friend called Christian who he goes clubbing with on Sunday nights in Vauxhall?'

And I said, 'Yes!'

And Uma laughs and says, 'There's a *powerful sexual chemistry* between you and Danny? The lad who uses the expensive moisturiser from House of Hardy? And is really into pop music?'

And I says, 'Yes, there is actually! He texts me loads! He says I'm the funniest girl he's met ever.' 'Oh, OK,' said Uma, and she was going to say something else but then she stopped. Oh god, Uma thinks he's well out of my league doesn't she? Oh god, even my mates think I ming big time.

LAST NIGHT WAS THE BLOODY HOUSE OF HARDY GROTTO CHRISTMAS PARTY. Oh god. Oh god. Oh bloody hell no no no. Why?!!! Why do human beings drink alcohol?? It should be BANNED! Banned by the government! And the Queen! And it especially should not be served at Christmas 'cos that's when you are a bit emotional and worrying about being single and worrying that no one fancies you and it makes you do the most stupid stuff EVER. Alcohol makes people who are MUNTERS suddenly well buff and it makes people who are dull as crap into the most interesting people ever. And MORE THAN ANYTHING it makes you forget that people are watching you so you totally don't care that you're dressed as an elf in stripy tights and a pointy hat, actually stood in the middle of the House of Hardy staff canteen which is now a temporary dance floor and you're actually DIRTY DANCING with Thor from the Outer Hebrides who is also dressed as an Elf and you've pushed his false nose to the side so you can snog him and he's kissing your neck and you're shutting your eyes and going 'Ooh ahhh ooooh!' and making a raunchy face while everyone else is dancing to *Living La Vida Loca* by Ricky Martin and laughing their heads off around you.

And alcohol totally makes you NOT realise that one of the other elves is filming it all on their phone with a plan

to put it up on YouTube and then email the link to everyone on the staff mailing list in House of Hardy with the title 'Warning: May Contain Elf Porn'.

AAAAAAAAAAAAAAAAAAAAAAAAAAAAAAAAAAGH!

THAT BLOODY MULLED WINE STUFF SHOULD BE BANNED! IT IS MULLED BY SATAN IN HIS FIERY PIT.

THURSDAY 24TH DECEMBER

LAST DAY IN THE GROTTO. I said goodbye to SC tonight. And I nearly started crying! What a silly cow!!? SC was sitting on his little seat when I popped my head round the door and said bye. 'Shiraz Bailey Wood!' he says. 'Thank you for all of your hard work! I hope I manage to bring the gifts you want this Christmas!'

So I giggled, remembering our funny conversation that time and said, 'When you setting off on your rounds then SC?'

And SC looked at his watch and said, 'Oh, soon, soon, I'll drink this tea first. I'll not get a hot drink all night. Everyone leaves me whisky! And I can't touch a drop. Not when I've got the sleigh!'

So I laughed again and said, 'Well hope it goes OK anyway!'

And he says, 'Thank you!'

So I looked at him and I don't know what come over me 'cos I tried not to say it but I couldn't help it, and then I said, "'Ere SC . . . are you, y'know . . . real?' And I felt proper stupid saying it.

So SC laughed and he said, 'Well, do you believe in me?'

And I blushed and said, 'Well I didn't. But I sort of do now!'

And SC smiled his twinkly SC smile and said, 'Well that's good because only people who believe get the presents they want! Merry Christmas Shiraz!' So I closed the door and walked out and I had a little tear in my eye for some stupid reason and bloody hell I'm glad I've left the grotto because I think it's sent me a little bit mad. Good mad, but still mad.

And then I got to the locker room and Ritu was packing her bag to leave and I said, 'When does your flight to Japan leave, Ritu?'

And she says, 'Oh not till December 27th from Gatwick.' And then Ritu told me she was spending Christmas Day all on her own in her house in Kensington 'cos all her flatmates had flown home already! So I invited her to Goodmayes to experience a real, live Essex Christmas. And she said yes! So I rang my mother and told her a Japanese person was coming and she said, 'Ooh blimey they eat dog at Christmas don't they?! Or is that Korea? Korea is in China isn't it? Well she ain't eating our Penny! I'll get in some of them Supernoodles! Chinese love noodles don't they?'

I tried to explain to my mum that Japan, China and

Korea were all different places but she couldn't quite grasp it. Right, that's everything packed. Time to meet Ritu at Liverpool Street station. HAPPY CHRISTMAS!

CHRISTMAS DAY – FRIDAY 25TH DECEMBER

Hahhahhahahhhhhhhhaaa big up da Wooodzzzz! Woot woot! This is how we roll at Christmas time!! LULZZZZ, ha ha ha ha! I luv these peeps so much. Oh too tired to write now. And too full. Laterzzzzzzshizzlebizzlewood xxxxx

SATURDAY 26TH DECEMBER

Well I reckon Ritu has experienced a full Essex Christmas in all of its glory. We got the last train to Goodmayes on Christmas Eve with all the pissheads and crying girls and men wearing comedy antlers with vomit down their jackets which Ritu thought was very exciting. Then we went back to Thundersley Road and we sat up with my mother and cuddled little Fin who is even bigger and even angrier looking than ever. 'She's got herself a squawker here,' my mother said, trying to stop Fin crying, but he seemed to be enjoying himself too much. Cava-Sue looked knackered. It was like she didn't even know it was Christmas at all. Then we drank blue WKD and ate mint Matchmakers and we watched carols on BBC1 and taught Ritu the rude version of *Ding Dong Merrily on High*.

Then me and Ritu crashed out but about six hours later everyone was up again; Lewis, Cava-Sue, Murphy, Dad and Mum, Rita and me all hanging out in our pyjamas dancing to *I Wish It Could Be Christmas Every Day* by Slade on Radio Essex and drinking fizzy wine and opening our pressies. SC never managed to get me that hot new media job in London but he did get me a Top Shop voucher and a Mac Cosmetics gift box. That was just as good really.

And as usual we all got tipsy too early. And Dad did his first 'Elvis on the toilet' impression by 11am and Ritu nearly died laughing. Then we pulled crackers and wore stupid paper hats and eventually Cava-Sue, who was supposed to be breastfeeding, had a large Baileys 'cos she said if she didn't get a drink she was going to sell Fin on bloody eBay as he was doing her head in screaming.

Then we gave Ritu her first Terry's Chocolate Orange and let her open the new tin of Quality Street and have her first green triangle. And normally Murphy moans if someone eats all the triangles but with Ritu he didn't mind. And then Murphy opened the aftershave I'd bought him from House of Hardy and he put some on and Ritu said, 'It very sexy smell.' And Murphy suddenly seemed about two feet taller and said he would show Ritu how to play his new PS3 game *Killerblow Karate* which they played for three hours and Ritu kept kicking his ass but then she is Japanese so we reckon kicking ass martial arts stylee might be in her blood. Murphy was proper impressed.

Mum peeled enough potatoes for thirty people and Dad kept telling everyone how early he got up to do the turkey and by the time Nan and Clement arrived everyone was actually a bit steaming. Clement brought his usual bottle of rum and him and Dad got stuck in having a wee nip to 'taste its constitution' then they both began yaddering on about Formula One racing and Mum told them off for not keeping an eye on 'the bird' which now looked a bit overdone.

We all ate dinner round the table in the kitchen and even though it folds to fit guests it was still totally too small. And we were all on chairs and stools at different levels and Murphy was on an Asda deckchair with his dinner on his knee. And we all ate ourselves silly. Even Ritu ate loads and she has never really eaten stuffing or chipolata sausage wrapped with bacon before. And after we'd had Christmas pudding with custard AND whipped cream, Ritu threw her hands over her mouth and tried not to burp but did anyway and then everyone cheered and gave her a clap. We made Ritu watch the Queen's speech and *Only Fools and Horses* and we all ate more chocolate tree decorations and drank more Baileys then we ate ham and piccalilli sandwiches and we played Monopoly and everyone stole from the bank at some point and then we started drinking flaming Sambucas and Lewis set light to his fringe by accident.

Then Dad put his *Best of Level-42* record on and we all had a dance and we were all being proper silly and even

more tipsy and even Cava-Sue was laughing and my
mother was doing her hands in the air dancing and at
some point at about 10pm I walked into the kitchen and
found Ritu and my brother in the dark by the sink
snogging each other's faces off!!! OH MY GOD! He's
sixteen and she is like eighteen!! And then Wesley called
and asked me to go out with him on New Year's Eve. And
Uma texted from her dad's in Portsmouth and Carrie
rang from the Dominican sounding hammered on
tequila. I can't really remember coming to bed, but me
and Ritu slept top and tail in my old single bed and when
I woke up we both still had our paper hats on and all our
clothes and bad heads and we both burst out laughing.

I think it was maybe the best Christmas day ever. Ritu
from Osaka in Japan definitely thought it was.

Oh god that reminds me – I wonder what I said to
Wesley?

JANUARY

FRIDAY IST JANUARY

It's a new year! And a new Shiraz Bailey Wood! OK, probably not a new one, but a more determined one who knows her own mind and knows what she wants and knows who she is and knows other stuff that sounds like the first verse from a Bcyoncé Knowles song.

And this year I am definitely not to be confused with the wishy-washy Shiraz who's a bit vacant about where she's going and ends up dressed as an elf in stripy tights padding about in an enchanted forest that is half waterlogged with kiddy's urine. Not that I regret being a Christmas elf or nothing, no. But it wasn't really getting me anywhere was it? Well except one step closer each day to having feet which actually were the same shape as the curly bloody slippers.

But I met some proper nice people at House of Hardy, Thor and Petra and Ritu and Reuben. Life in London definitely got better. And Uma is here with me now too! London is much better when you've got friends, 'cos the city is really expensive. You need people you can just have a laugh with 'cos having a laugh costs nothing at all. Walking down the street pointing at funny stuff and hanging round each other's flats costs jack don't it? I wish

Carrie could see that sometimes. These days she only thinks something is good if it's well expensive. Like last night, New Year's Eve, Carrie wanted to go to this VIP party at the Club Mystique in Mayfair. All the Butterz Beauty girls were going. I didn't fancy it myself. They're a right bunch of airheads. Who in their right minds would let any of those girls near their lady garden with hot wax and a spatula is beyond me. But anyway, tickets plus drinks plus taxis home plus an outfit was together all going to cost a bomb! So Carrie got all glammed up like Fashion Fever Barbie and spent almost one hundred and fifty quid going to Mystique and I went down by the River Thames with Thor and Ritu and Petra and a load of other people and we just wrapped up in loads of scarves and hats and took a bottle of Bacardi and watched this massive fireworks display by the London Eye with hundreds of thousands of tourists from all over the bloody world. And as Big Ben struck midnight for New Year it was proper incredible and the sky lit up with explosions and flashes and rockets and everyone was kissing and hugging each other. Well everyone except me and Thor who are totally pretending the Elf Porn YouTube business didn't happen. But anyway, it was a brilliant night and I will remember it for ever and it didn't cost anything really.

I had a brilliant New Year's Eve. I feel a bit bad 'cos Wesley Barrington Bains II had asked me if I wanted to go to a party with him in Goodmayes at this girl called Susan

Douvall's house. And when I was tipsy on Christmas Day I sort of said yes. But a few days ago I decided to go back to London instead 'cos to be honest all Fin's screaming was doing my head in. Wesley said he understood and he'd just go with Bezzie Kelleher. And I rang Wesley at midnight last night to say Happy New Year and I reckon he was having a good time anyhow. He couldn't get me off the phone quick enough. And I could hear girls screaming and laughing in the background and he sounded all tipsy and that. Which is good. I hope he had a good time and wasn't like thinking about me and him all the time or anything.

11pm – Hang on. 'Susan Douvall'? Is that THAT Sooz who used to work in Boots in Ilford? Sooz – that grumpy-looking cow who always used to fancy him? It's that Sooz isn't it? It's that bloody Sooz?

11.30pm – Have just rung Wesley. His phone is off. He must have a really bad hangover. I sent him a text saying HAPPY NEW YEAR. With two xxs. And a TEXT ME BACK PLEASE. He hasn't texted me back.

SATURDAY 2ND JANUARY

Today was a good day. It was Uma's day off from the casino and although it was frosty the sky was still well bright, so we wrapped up warm in jeans and tights and big hoodies and scarves and took Zeus for a walk in Victoria Park in East London. It's bare jokes going out with Zeus as he's just a big daft dog who wouldn't really hurt anyone, especially not a child 'cos he loves kids and just wants to wash them. 'Sadly, however, Zeus has been afflicted with an unfortunate tone of face which suggests he is a psychotic hound from hell who will rip your still-beating heart from your chest and eat it as a light pre-dinner snack.' That's what snooty Josh Fallow said back at Mayflower anyhow. People are definitely prejudicial and stigmatising towards brindle Staffordshire bull terriers with studded collars.

Saying that, one good thing about being with Zeus is you don't get any hassle either. Like from those crackheads in the park who wander around London scamming folk by pretending their cars have broken down and they need money for petrol, and they're well convincing 'cos they start pretending to cry and sometimes saying that their wife is dying in hospital and they just need a quid to get to her deathbed! Well it actually turns out it's just a con and they haven't even got a car or a wife they just need to find six different fools like Shiraz Bailey Wood to give them a pound coin each and then they can buy more crack! Well anyway, when you're with Zeus, you are a proper crackhead-free zone. Zeus is like the anti-crackhead machine. Crackheads run in the total opposite direction as fast as their scabby crackhead legs will carry them.

Uma has had a funny old Christmas. She went to see her dad in Portsmouth. He's out of jail now and reckons he's on the straight and narrow. So Uma's sort-of-stepmum, Mica, takes Uma to one side and begged her not to mention anything about that 'friend' Ricardo being around the house last month. Well this put Uma in a bit of a predicament 'cos Uma didn't want to tell her dad about Ricardo 'cos she could see he was on an even keel, but she didn't want to lie to him neither 'cos she loves her dad. So after a few days Uma just escaped back to London. Besides, she's had a prison visiting order through from Chelmsford Jail to visit her brother Clinton.

I asked Uma how Clinton was and Uma says, 'Oh y'know. The usual how he always is in jail. Crying. Crying like a girl. Crying about how he's locked up with nutters all day long. Moaning about the toilets. Moaning on about how he thinks he's gonna catch AIDS in there as people leave needles lying about. Moaning about how the best years of his life are passing him by and it's everyone else's fault but his own. Going up the wall basically.'

Then Uma lit up another Embassy Red and blew the smoke in a big jet out of her mouth 'cos the middle of the park was probably the only place left now she can legally enjoy a fag in London. 'Thing is Shiz, Clinton always wanted to be a gangster. He always wanted to be a big man,' Uma says. 'Always. Even when he was tiny he wanted to be a rudeboy. Well good for him, now he is one. Proper big man. Locked up twenty-two hours a day. With his little sister buying him his Haribo sweets and toilet rolls and taking him in books to read that are for like ten-year-old kids 'cos he's been sitting about doing jack for eight years and he can't even hardly bloody read 'cos he never went to school.' Then Uma pinged her fag end into the middle of nowhere and we walked home. Uma didn't sound upset about it or nothing. She sounded proper calm. I couldn't imagine what I'd be like if our Murphy was in that position. I'd have a bloody nervous breakdown, I reckon.

Tonight me and Uma went to see this thing called The Nutcracker. It was a ballet. A ballet at a big posh theatre in the West End performed by these geezers from Russia called The Moscow Ballet. One of Uma's best customers at the Imperial Palace left Uma some tickets on the door as a present!! I've never been to a ballet before. It was the most brilliant thing ever. The theatre was full of loads and loads of rich people all in rows on purple velvet seats. I reckoned the ballet would be quite dull, just anorexic birds in flouncy skirts running about on their toes for three hours but it wasn't like that at all.

It had all different songs and a proper story and dancers dressed up as Christmas presents and Christmas puddings and mice and it honestly was totally brilliant and it gave me bumps all over my arms and neck. Especially when some of the boys and girls came out just in twos and did their dances together. Me and Uma never said a single word right the way through and when I looked over at Uma at one point when the Sugarplum

Fairy was dancing to this plinkyplonky music I realised Uma was having a little cry. But I knew she didn't want me to know so I pretended not to see.

MONDAY 4TH JANUARY

Oh my god. I just had a text from Danny at Working Magic. He reckons he's got me a media type job. Something to do with newspapers. I have to go and see him tomorrrow! Thank you Danny! And more to the point THANK YOU SC OVER IN LAPLAND! I KNEW YOU WOULDN'T LET ME DOWN!!!

WEDNESDAY 6TH JANUARY

Mmmmmmm OK. Right. This ain't exactly the job what I was dreaming of but it's a job and I am skint so WHATEVER. My new job for the next four weeks is giving out *London Alive* free newspapers in Trafalgar Square. It's only for four hours a day and they pay you by the day so I can't really say no can I? It's regular money. I got home tonight and passed Uma just off out to work and I told her and she sort of giggled and said, 'Oh well, it's a start ain't it? Everyone's got to start somewhere!' So I laughed but then I realised she wasn't joking. Uma does think that standing in the street giving out free papers is the first stage to a fantastic media job. The thing is, with her, it probably would be.

Oh god. This paper thing is proper miserable. I ain't feeling it at all.

I have to stand in the middle of Trafalgar Square wearing a bright orange coat and a bright orange hat and orange trousers that are too big for me and I have to carry a great big pile of *London Alive*s and basically try to jam them into people's hands as they walk by. And most people give you a big body swerve like you're covered in dog poo and flies or something. And some people pretend you're invisible. In fact you start slapping yourself sometimes to double check you're not. And some people get proper confused and angry and shout 'I don't want to buy anything from you!' And some people start yelling at you about the environmental impact of giving out free newspapers like it's bloody me that's personally got me foot on a polar bear's head drowning it while melting the snow caps with me own bloody hairdryer.

And some people just throw the newspapers right on the ground in front of you which is annoying 'cos you've got to pick them up again and try and make them look straight again. And you have to give out at least two thousand papers a day or else they basically take back their orange gimp suit and you ain't got a job no more. And everyone in London is proper miserable in January. London's not all twinkly and exciting like it was in December. It's just cold and dark and wet all day and everyone's run up loads of debt on their credit card and have got faces like they're proper worried.

Sometimes I think London is just totally full of millions of people like me who can't afford to live here but can't work out where else to go 'cos once you've been here everywhere else feels well boring.

Oh Jesus thank god I don't actually work for the newspaper writing any of this crap down eh? Even my diary is so dull I feel like polishing my own face with a cheese grater.

SATURDAY 9TH JANUARY

10am – Our Murphy has gone missing! My mother just rang me now and asked to speak to him seeing as he was spending the weekend with me. I told her I didn't know nothing about it! So Mum starts panicking going, 'Oh my god then maybe he's ran away from home then!' So I says, 'Well have you done anything to upset him?' and Mum says, 'Nah, nothing. Well nothing really, I mean, he had the hump 'cos I tried to squeeze one of his spots, but it needed squeezing! I told him, "Murphy, I'm not sitting eating my chicken kiev with that bloody thing glowing at me!"'

So I says to my mum, 'Well it can't be that. He's used to that. We all squeeze his spots.'

Then Mum says, 'Yeah, I suppose, Shiraz. But he has been acting proper strange lately. Sort of giddy he is. And always on his mobile. And now he's bleeding vanished. Oh my god Shiraz what are we going to do! Shall I phone the police? Shall I get out his photo to give them?'

I told her to hang fire and I'd ring Tariq and see if he knew anything. Oh god I hope our Murphy is all right. I know he's a big tall lad with his pants pulled out of the back of his trousers but he's just a little boy really. He's really quite innocent. Oh no, I think I'm gonna have to say another prayer.

SUNDAY 10TH JANUARY

OK – let's call off the police helicopters and sniffer dogs, I've found my brother Murphy. And NO he hadn't been abducted by Albanian people-traffickers and sold for his kidneys. Oh no. Oh no no no no no no. HE WAS ROUND AT RITU'S FLAT IN KENSINGTON IN HER BED. They have been seeing each other on the sly since she got back from Japan in the New Year and not telling any of us. Bloody Ritu told me she's had flu for the last few days and literally couldn't stand up!! 'Oh I so sorry Shiraz!' Ritu kept saying today, 'I no want to put you in awkward position! I not know he not tell your mother!'

And when Murphy finally came to the phone, after a lot of nagging, y'know something? He didn't even sound sheepish! He sounded knackered and very very happy. 'Soz Shizza,' he says. 'It's proper noisy at home in Goodmayes what with Fin screaming and that and then

154

Ritu invited me to come and have a weekend of erm, chilling out and that. Get me, sis?'

I was trying to 'get him' but the image of what he was maybe getting up to was making small explosions of sick in my mouth. Anyway I've just rang my mother and said I've located Murphy and he's in good spirits. I fibbed and said he's now with me at my flat. I said Murphy would come back to Essex soon but he was proper fascinated in finding out about my job as an estate agent so it might not be till Tuesday. What an entire family of bloody liars we are.

'Oh, I don't know what to think, Shiraz,' my mother said. 'It seems like only yesterday he was happy playing out in the street, kicking his ball about!' I almost told her not to worry as he was now in an eighteen-year-old Japanese girl's bed getting a whole new type of exercise, but I couldn't face the bloody hassle.

TUESDAY 12TH JANUARY

Why isn't Wesley Barrington Bains II returning my calls? WHY? What's his problem? Has he got the hump with me or something? Wesley always texts me back. But now I don't get nothing back or I get a tiny little text that don't mean anything about five hours later. I know me and him have split up and that but he always answers my calls. That's Wesley. That's what Wesley does. I thought we were mates? God, I feel really single now. I didn't notice it so much in December when there was loads to do.

And of course Carrie isn't spending January single and lonely, is she? No Carrie has got a new boyfriend called Barclay. Barclay is a footballer. Barclay is a reserve for Southend. Carrie met Barclay at Mystique on New Year's Eve 'cos they were both in the Very Very VIP area and he bought her a glass of champagne and when they left together to go to the after-party the paparazzi took their photo 'cos they thought they were a proper famous couple! Carrie has told me that story two hundred and thirty-five times and bought every *Heat* magazine since but her and Barclay haven't been in. Probably 'cos they look like the Costcutter version of Posh and Becks, I reckon. Oh I don't mean that. I'm being a cow.

To be honest, Barclay is probably the most gorgeous man I have ever seen up close. He looks like he should be in a magazine Hunks in Trunks pull-out special. Barclay is about six foot one tall with a perfect toned body, short blond hair and pale blue eyes. On the other hand though, I reckon Barclay might be the stupidest person I think I have ever met. In fact I worry about him really. This morning I found him in the kitchen staring at the kettle for twenty minutes going, 'Mnnnnmm reckon it's broken. Mmmmnmnmnm. Is this fing broken? Shiz?' And then Uma walked in and plugged it in and made him a cuppa. It's like God put all his energy into making him sexy and then gave him a tiny weeny little brain the size of a Ferrero Rocher that can only think about kicking a football. Carrie is madly in love with him. Madly. There's a lot of screaming coming out of her bedroom right now. I reckon Barclay must tickle her a lot.

WEDNESDAY 13TH JANUARY

Carrie must be in a well good mood. She has agreed that Uma and Zeus can stay permanent! Uma is doing a lot of late shifts at the casino now so she can have my bed during the day and I sleep there at night. And Carrie's out loads anyway so it all works out OK. I am well happy about Uma staying. The flat is much better fun since she arrived. And Uma is proper clean and tidy so we always have clean plates and cups and don't find them under Carrie's bed covered in knickers and green mould no more. That is proper minging. And Uma can cook too so we have hot food now and then. The flat is quite funny at the moment. We're like a little family.

FRIDAY 15TH JANUARY

OK I did something a bit brave today. I was in Trafalgar Square starting my shift giving out *London Alive* when I got talking to Sophus, the guy who delivers them to my spot. Sophus delivers the papers in a big orange van every afternoon from the head offices in Wapping in East London. So anyway, Sophus was being all chatty today and he was saying that the *London Alive* head offices are well exciting 'cos they employ hundreds of people and there's always something happening like photo shoots, models arriving, celebs popping in, journalists coming and going. So I listened for a bit thinking how good that all sounded and suddenly I thought, what would Uma do right now? Well, Uma would be a bit pushy and ask for what she wanted wouldn't she?

So I takes a deep breath and says to Sophus, ''Ere Sophus, I live right near that factory. Is there any way I could meet you at Head Office on Monday morning and get a lift down with you to save my tube fare?' And Sophus shrugs and goes, 'Yeah, no problem Shiraz. You're not meant to go inside without a pass really but I can tell security to look out for you. See you at the warehouse at midday! Just come to the main gate and ask for Sophus and they'll let you in. Ooh you'll see some sights down there I tell you! It's a mad house.'

I'm not sure what the hell I'm doing but suddenly work on Monday seems like more fun.

SATURDAY 16TH JANUARY

I rang Cava-Sue today but she sounded really weird. Proper spaced out. Cava-Sue says she's taken Fin to Dr Gupta twice this week to find out why he makes a noise like a fire alarm all the time but Dr Gupta says there ain't anything wrong with Fin. Dr Gupta say that sometimes babies just scream 'cos they're going through a phase of screaming and that he'll grow out of it.

So Cava-Sue says, 'When?' and the doctor laughs and says, 'Who can tell? Next week? Next month? When he's four!?' Cava-Sue says she came home on the bus and she was so tired she fell asleep and missed Thundersley Road, then she jumped off the bus and forgot Fin in his pram and had to run alongside the bus to the next stop to collect him. This sounds like it would be proper funny if it was Steve-O and Johnny Knoxville doing it on *Jackass* but not when it's our Cava-Sue. I tried to talk to her more but Fin was screaming again so she hung up. Poor Cava-Sue. I don't know how I can help.

MONDAY 18TH JANUARY

When I said I lived right near the *London Alive* head office I was totally not keeping it real at all. It's about two miles away. Luckily Uma has totally worked out how to get free wi-fi from the neighbours so I borrowed Carrie's Macbook and went on to www.magicmaps.co.uk and found the directions. The *London Alive* office was right near a tube stop on the East London line. I've never been down that bit of London before and I felt a bit scared but I tried to look at it as an adventure, not something that was bound to fail before it even started. I packed my orange goon outfit in a bag and dressed in black with quite neutral make-up.

I got to *London Alive* at about 11am and I wasn't

meeting Sophus for an hour, but the security guards let me in anyway. So I wandered through the gates up to the front of the building. It felt pretty exciting just being there. There were all sorts of journalistic types looking all tired and weaselly, stood outside reception smoking fags and gossiping about news stories. And two very tall, thin women wearing dark glasses were looking at a piece of paper, arguing over a headline about skirts. And just that minute a white van arrived and a whole rack of clothes was being transported around the side of the building. And as I walked closer one man came running out of the reception shouting, 'There's going to be a press conference at Westminster at 1pm! The idiot is resigning from cabinet at last!' and then all the weaselly-looking folk who were smoking stubbed their fags out and ran back inside and I was thinking, 'Bloody hell I don't even know what's going on but this is already more bloody exciting than giving the papers out at Trafalgar Square.'

So I walks round the side of the building where Sophus's van was parked, but there was no sign of Sophus. And that's where I saw a big set of doors where all the racks of clothes and bags of mail were being pushed through, marked GOODS IN. So I wandered through that door and inside there was about fifty blokes in blue trousers and blue T-shirts all running about like crazy wearing headsets, picking up boxes and ticking them off lists then disappearing off through another set of doors where I couldn't see. And standing on a raised platform was this big white-haired bloke who was about fifty with a headset on who looked like he was in charge. 'You lost, darling?' he shouts.

So I jumped a bit 'cos I knew I was out of order being there and I said, 'Ooh, yeah, I'm a bit lost I reckon. Which department is this?'

'This is the Goods-In section, sweetheart,' he said. 'This is where all the postal and despatch deliveries for the newspaper staff arrive. And then my post-boys sort them and take them to the journalists' desks for them.'

'Oh,' I said, watching this rack of clothes disappearing away through some swing doors. 'So, like, that rack of clothes? Are they for the *What to Wear Right Now* pages on eight and nine!?' So the man laughs and said, 'Exactamundo me lovely. Those clothes are exactly what to wear right now. Well, more like What to Wear Right Tomorrow' 'cos they haven't been delivered to the fashion team for them to decide on yet. But yeah, what you have there is tomorrow's fashion column, right in front of your eyes!'

This felt amazing. I felt proper giddy. And I didn't know why but the only thing I did know was that I didn't want to leave. So I tried to think quick, then I took a deep breath and then I said what I knew Uma would say if she was in exactly this position. 'Anyway,' I says to the bloke, pulling back my shoulders and trying to look like I was meant to be there, 'I'm Shiraz Bailey Wood. I've been sent by Working Magic. I've come about the job.'

TUESDAY 19TH JANUARY

Today was my first day working in the postroom of the *London Alive* head office! I'm a post-boy! Or, as I pointed out to Mr Whitworth who runs the Goods-in department, I'm a post-person. And Mr Whitworth laughed when I said that and said well he'd never had to bother with all that 'post-person/post-boy' politically correct nonsense before 'cos you don't ever get any girls who want to work in the postroom. Only boys will do the job.

'Well I'm the girl who will change all that,' I says to him!

And he laughs and said he didn't know where the hell I'd come from 'cos he'd not asked Working Magic to send no one and he thought I was probably a bit of a nutter, but I was a nutter from Goodmayes in Essex and that was where his old granny was from so he decided to give me the job going 'cos all people from Goodmayes are 'honest, decent sorts'. I decided not to tell Mr Whitworth about Clinton being on remand for the kilo of cocaine. I didn't want to disappoint him.

I have spent the entire day running round the *London Alive* offices delivering parcels. I've been to the fashion department where all the tall women with dark glasses sit and the travel section where this sunburnt bloke with a beard sits reading a book about Africa all day long. And I've been to the newsroom which is full of men swearing at each other and throwing pens at each other. And this afternoon I've been about six times to the advertising section which is full of cocky, noisy folk in headsets shouting about money. And finally today I went to the features department which is full of bored-looking posh women talking about whether they should do articles about 'wheat allergies' or 'should you have a baby after the age of forty-five'. And I actually heard one woman in the features department called Petula telling another called Mariella that it was time to ring Kitten Montague-Jones and chase her for this week's Kitten's Titbits column which was late AGAIN.

How funny is that eh? Kitten Montague-Jones doesn't even remember to hand her column in! Someone has to ring her and remind her. And she gets away with it 'cos her dad plays golf with the managing editor. I wish my dad played golf with the managing editor of a company. My dad plays darts with a bloke called Lonny who is a binman so maybe he could have pulled strings there.

11pm – Actually, I don't reckon Dad plays darts with Lonny no more. I reckon Lonny was the one who got banned for getting drunk and weeing against the bar. Never mind. Another door closes.

THURSDAY 21ST JANUARY

I'm really enjoying this new job. It's always busy and the other boys are proper nice to me and we have a laugh. I like boys' sense of humour. It's just rude and silly and you know where you stand. Just like the laughs me and our Murphy used to have. Or me and Wesley. Well, before Wesley started blanking my calls. Not that I'm bothered. If Wesley wants space he can have as much as he likes. All the space from here to Essex. Suits me. Whatever.

I was telling Uma about *London Alive* tonight when we were lying on the couch with Zeus on top of us keeping us warm, so we don't need to bother with the radiators being on. 'That's proper good y'know Shiz,' Uma says. 'Loads of important folk start off in the postroom at places! You could be like editor of the whole place one day. Shiraz Bossman!'

'Yeah, bare jokes,' I said, rubbing Zeus's ears.

So we lay there for a bit and then Uma says, 'No Shiz, you wanna drop your curriculum vitae thing off on some of the desks on your way round and see if they need anyone to do a bit of writing. You're well good at writing, you are! Remember when you used to always write the scripts and stuff for the Mayflower Winter Festival?'

'Yeah, Uma,' I says, 'and I remember you burning the assembly hall down during the Year Ten Winter Festival.'

Uma rolled her eyes a bit and laughed. 'That weren't strictly me was it? That was Latoya Bell.'

'No, it was you, Uma,' I said. Uma just shakes her head as if she's having trouble remembering.

'Oh bloody hell! My memory is well bad!' says Uma. 'But anyway Shiraz I'm being serious! Give them your CV!

Someone's got to do these jobs, it may as well be folk like you and me!'

Then Uma gets all serious and tuts and says, 'Shiz, have you even got a CV to give to those features desk thingy people?' So I says no, but I have got a copy of that form I filled in last August for Working Magic. So I goes and gets it and Uma read it and then she started laughing. And laughing. And laughing so much I thought she was going to actually fall off the sofa. 'Have you any office experience? Answer: Yes, I have experience of sitting in our headmaster Mr Bamblebury's office on many occasions!!!' Ha ha ha ha ha!' Uma was howling. I couldn't really see what was that funny.

Uma is going to help me write my curriculum vitae. She says keeping it real sometimes ain't doing me any favours.

FRIDAY 22ND JANUARY

Oh god. Wesley Barrington Bains II is going out with Susan Douvall. Sooz. Bloody Sooz. He's PROPERLY going out with her. Like they are properly a couple. Like people actually say, 'Oh are Wesley and Susan coming out tonight?' like once they used to say 'Wesley and Shiraz'. Oh bloody hell. No. And she's been to his house and met his mum and everything. I can't believe this. We've only been split up like six months! And I'm not seeing anyone! I mean, OK I got off with Thor and I fancy

Danny and there was that time I had that fling with Joshua Fallow BUT that doesn't matter 'cos this is different! This is like a whole new relationship. Our Murphy told me about it tonight on the phone. He saw them going into Halfords. WESLEY TAKES SOOZ TO HALFORDS! THAT'S WHERE HE USED TO TAKE ME!

So I rang Wesley tonight to ask why he doesn't send me any funny texts any more and he sounded sort of weird then he says, 'It's difficult now Shiraz, innit.'

So I says, 'So you don't want to be friends with me now you're with Sooz then?'

And he says, 'No, it's not like that, innit. It's just Sooz thinks it's a bit weird, innit.'

And I felt my throat go all crackly and I said, 'How is it weird!!?' And he went all quiet and then I could hear Sooz kicking off in the background and my name being said then he hung up. I don't know why I'm even upset. I keep thinking about her sniffing his Kouros aftershave and kissing his neck and I feel like I want to be sick.

I put my new Uma-style CV on all the desks in the features department at *London Alive* today when all the posh bored-looking women were in a meeting. Then I ran into the editor's office and put one on her desk too. She is this big dark-haired scary lady called Georgina. Nothing will ever come of it. NOTHING. My entire life is just a bloody laughable string of failure, disappointment and missed opportunity and I am destined to die in an old folks' home with no children, no grandchildren or husband who even cares about me and instead a huge angry nurse who I pay all my savings to will wipe my bum and feed me my tapioca. I told Uma this tonight and she just laughed her head off and blew Embassy Red smoke down both nostrils like a dragon and said, 'Oh give it a rest, Shiraz, you silly cow! Ha ha ha ha!'

FEBRUARY

TUESDAY 2ND FEBRUARY

I always say that living in London sometimes feels like being invisible, well it's really like that at *London Alive* 'cos you can go for days sometimes without anyone in the main editorial building even acknowledging you exist. Especially the women in the features department – Petula and Mariella and this other skinny woman in thick dark glasses called Phoebe. When I come to pick up their mail they just carry on their conversations like I'm not there at all.

It's weird 'cos it's like just 'cos I'm wearing navy blue trousers and a blue baseball hat and a blue T-shirt it means I'm just not on their level so they reckon I can't hear them moaning about finding a Spearmint Rhino lapdancing-joint receipt on their husband's credit card. Or how they've just got sixty per cent off Manolo Blahnik shoes at House of Hardy by pretending to be someone in the fashion team who died last year of anorexia. And even sometimes when I start laughing by accident they don't even notice I'm standing right there. In fact the only time they ever mention any of us in the postroom is any time anything goes missing, then they say stuff like, 'Oh my god, my handbag is missing! I've lost my other

Tiffany earring! Where's my laptop? It must be the post-boys! Or the cleaners! We've no idea who they are really! They're from some terrible estates. They're a right load of chavs!' then about four minutes later all their panic is over 'cos Petula's found her lost earring under a big pile of coffee cups and party invitations on her desk. It's quite good being invisible though 'cos it's proper amazing seeing how *London Alive* is put together. I love it how random things that people mention in the office when they're having a coffee start to grow into a big story that ends up in the paper. Like one minute they're talking about some bit of celebrity gossip and the next thing they've made a whole double page out of it with pictures and everything!

Well anyway, today something hilarious happened and I don't know if I've got the guts to front this one out but I've told Uma about it and she says she's gonna drop my ass to the kerb if I don't. So today I was floating invisibly like a ghost through the features department going to pick up a parcel what Mariella was sending back to Italy when all of a sudden Petula with the mousy bobbed hair said, 'Oh drat, I've just had some bad news about our work experience intern, Tiffany! She's cancelled on us. She's going to dig a well in Mozambique for an AIDS charity instead.'

So Mariella with the pointy nose and big lips what looks a bit like one of the Riddlers says, 'Oh that is a shame isn't it! Tiffany is a dear! She's the head of advertising's daughter isn't she? We've had that internship pencilled into the diary for two years! What will we do now?' So then Mariella frowns and says, 'Mmmmm nightmare, that leaves us with a gap of nobody making the coffee and doing all the faffy paperwork stuff for like SIX weeks or something? Can't we get another intern girl from somewhere? I mean we do pay a small amount of money don't we?'

They both sat trying to use their collective brain power. I'm sure I could hear clanking. 'Aren't any of our other friends' daughters free?' Mariella said, going through her address book. Petula got her electronic personal organiser thingy out too. So the two women sat there for a bit shouting hilarious names like 'Persephone?' 'What about Magdalene?' 'What about Zaza?' Until eventually the door swings open on the little private office that the editor Georgina sits in and this scary woman peers out and says in a loud northern voice, 'Why don't you two go and get that big pile of CVs and choose someone who you don't know for a change?'

Well Petula and Mariella didn't look very happy about that. 'Pah, she would say that!' hissed Mariella. 'She'd have the place overrun with chavs if she could. Her and her equal opportunities, jobs for yobs ideas!' And then Petula whispered loudly, 'Oh god, well Georgina is no better than a chav herself. She came from the bottom, that one, and I can't wait till she shuffles off back!' But they were obviously a bit scared of Georgina so Mariella went and got a pile of CVs and started looking through. Well the very first one she picked up she started laughing. 'SHIRAZ BAILEY WOOD!' Mariella was sneering.

'SHIRAZ BAILEY WOOD?' repeats Petula. 'What? Shiraz, as in the wine? And Bailey as in that stuff that pikeys drink at Christmas?!' The pair sat cackling for a bit as I stood proper still with sweat dripping inside my navy blue sweatshirt and my hair all sticky under my baseball hat. They were making me feel terrible. Just like Joshua Fallow's mother did that time. Why do some people think they are so much better than you?

'Actually this is a very good CV!' said Mariella, sounding shocked. 'She was head girl at Mayflower Ladies Academy! She can type one hundred and twenty words per minute and she speaks fluent French, German and conversational Arabic.' OH MY DAYS, I knew Uma shouldn't have bloody put Arabic. Then Georgina appeared again out of her office looking like she was going to open a big can of northern woman whoop ass and said, 'Shiraz Bailey Wood? I love it. She sounds perfect. Call her now.'

Seconds later my phone started to vibrate in my pocket, so I ran into the stationery cupboard and answered it. I could hardly speak I was shaking so much. All I remember saying again and again was that I'd start as soon as possible.

Mr Whitworth has been proper understanding about me leaving the postroom. He thinks it is hilarious that I'm going up to Features to do an internship. Mr Whitworth says he's told his mate Sophus who drives the vans and he sent me a message saying, 'Good on you girl!'

I went for my first day today. When I first got here this morning everyone stared at my pink hoodie and my scrunchie and my hoops like I was in bloody fancy dress or something and then Mabel in the fashion department said I was very 'ghetto chic' and everyone agreed and nodded like that was a good thing and then I went invisible again. It was all a bit weird 'cos now I'm working in Features I am a whole different type of being invisible. I am only invisible now like eighty per cent of the time and the other twenty per cent, when anyone wants anything crap doing, they are very very very nice to me like I am dying of leukaemia or something. So they blank me from say 10am until lunchtime and then suddenly at 11.55am Mariella goes, 'Shiiiiiiiiiirrrrrrraz? Darling! Can you go and get us some organic salad boxes and drinks from the delicatessen?' And then off I skip with twenty quid in my hand and pick up their dry cleaning on the way, leaving them sitting at their desks mumbling away about 'global warming' and how they should maybe do another feature telling everyone to stop flushing their toilets as much and make their own human poo manure pile in their garden instead.

Anyway, the best bit of today was at about 4pm when Mariella says, 'Shiiiiiiiiiraaz? My angel! Could you give Kitten Montague-Jones a call and get her column from her?' So I says, 'Oh OK, no problem. Do I just remind her and then she emails it over to me?' Well everyone laughed then. 'No darling,' said Mariella. 'Kitten doesn't actually *write* the column. Just ring her and get her ideas down. Kitten just adds the, y'know, vibes. That's her phone number.'

So I call the number on the Post-it note and I can't believe I'm going to be chatting to the famous It Girl Kitten Montague-Jones!! And Kitten's phone rings for a bit and then eventually this voice that's obviously totally just woken up goes, 'Yeaaaah?' and I say, 'Hello, I'm Shiraz Bailey Wood calling from *London Alive*!' And this really confused croaky voice says, 'You're what? You're standing in a wood but you're still alive?'

So I said my name again and then Kitten just sighs loudly and said, 'Oh yeah, OK, erm . . . hang on, you've got a pen yeah?' Then I could hear her blowing her nose into a tissue and coughing a bit and her other phone ringing and her shouting at a maid or someone to make her a coffee. 'Erm right, OK, so, ummm, yeah, can you just say, like, red, Bazzatyne Storm. Erm, bubble, bubblesomething hairgloss party? It was in a museum somewhere. They had oysters. Or something. I don't bloody know. Oh I was with Stark. Stark Mazoor. Are you writing all this down as I'm not repeating it. Yeah it was a good night. Look that's it. That's all I can do. I'm too tired. And could you bloody tell Mariella that I clearly said 5pm today. Don't wake me up again.' Then she put the phone down without saying goodbye. Cheeky cow.

I looked at all the notes but they didn't make any bloody sense at all. So I went and left them on Mariella's desk and sat and waited to be fired for being the most rubbish intern ever. But somehow I wasn't.

FRIDAY 5TH FEBRUARY

KITTEN'S TITBITS HOT PARTY GOSSIP
FROM OUR VERY OWN IT GIRL

Mwah mwah dahlinks! Yes, it's your very own Kitten Montague-Jones reporting on another hectic week of fabby showbiz parties. Wowzers . . . Kitten's kitten-heels have hardly touched the ground this week. It's been a celebbytastic seven days.

For me, the highlight was Tuesday night. So many of my close personal A-list friends were on the red carpet for the BubblesBeautiful Hairgloss launch party at the Victoria and Albert Museum! Justin Le Grand flew in from Miami to DJ. And Stark Mazoor was my date. Stark is SUCH a mega-hottie. And he just adored my new red Bazzatyne Storm dress that Bazzatyne made me especially for the party! What a fabulous night! I think I may have overindulged on all the oysters and Moët. I'm a tiny bit delicate. Stay beautiful, my smitten kitten fans – love you all madly – KM-Jxxxxxx

SATURDAY 6TH FEBRUARY

I'm a bit hacked off with Carrie. OK, *well* hacked off. I don't want to have a big old bust up with her or nothing 'cos she has been my bezzie mate since we were like Year Seven or something but I just reckon she's changing right before my eyes into someone I ain't really that fond of.

But then maybe I'm changing too 'cos once upon a time I'd have fronted up and said all this right to her face and kept it totally real. I wouldn't have just written it all in my diary and then been nice to her face like a faker just 'cos I need somewhere to live. Oh my life! I reckon London is changing us both into different people and I'm the only one who sees it. Sometimes I wonder if we can even carry on being friends.

It's just that this week Carrie hasn't even really noticed that I've been working in the *London Alive* features department. And I reckon it's a proper big deal and she should be proud! And when I told her that Kitten Montague-Jones don't even write that Kitten's Titbits bloody column, Mariella does, well Carrie looked at me like I was lying or something and then started sticking up for Kitten and saying, 'Oh well I was at that BubbleBeautiful Hairgloss party and it *was* amazing! So what's untrue about that?'

And then I told her that Sean Burton who we went to school with had sent me an email and Carrie wasn't even that interested. This is Sean Burton! Sean who was like our really good friend at Mayflower! We were some of the very first people ever who he told he fancied boys not girls! Our friend from Goodmayes, Sean! So I told Carrie that Sean said he was going to visit us soon, well she sort of acted like he was someone from the distant past who she hardly remembered! And then, WELL THE WORST BIT WAS, I told her I was proper worried about our Cava-Sue as Mum reckons she's stopped talking and keeps crying all the time and Carrie looks at me, proper distracted by the telly and says, 'Oh yeah, how is Flint?' FLINT!!!! How is my nephew FLINT? Does she mean Fin?

Carrie, bruv, you have CHANGED. You better know yourself little girl! And by the way, your boyfriend Barclay is so bloody thick that I found him yesterday morning lying on the bedroom floor nearly crying 'cos he'd put both legs down the same leg of his boxer shorts and fell over! WHAT A CHUMP! And me and Uma have this joke where we say we are always proper relieved when he's in the flat 'cos at least we know where he is and he's safe and he's not wandering about in the moving traffic or anything. Ha ha ha ha LMAO! This is Shiraz Bailey Wood signing out at *keepingitreal.com*

THURSDAY 11TH FEBRUARY

Today was a bit weird, 'cos I got up and had a bit of a run in with Carrie 'cos I'd borrowed her GHDs and given them back with the gas canister nearly run down. And she'd got the hump so I stuck them outside her door and banged on it proper loud then she stormed out to college and I couldn't find any clean clothes to wear so I was late for work.

And I'd hardly got in the office and hung my hoodie up when the phone starts ringing and it was Mariella saying that there had been a DISASTER! Mariella reckons she had eaten something last night at a restaurant and that she had been totally poisoned as it not only contained wheat but it contained milk too and she is strictly and dangerously lactose as well as wheat intolerant. Well I was going to give her my little speech about Africans with flies all over their heads not saying no to cheese poonanis but somehow I kept my gob shut.

So then Mariella says, 'Can you write up Kitten's notes into a column? They're on a Post-it note stuck on to my Mac screen. You've written before haven't you

Shiraz? Your CV says you won the *Cosmopolitan* Junior Journalist competition?'

OH MY LIFE – I really will have to double-check all the stuff that Uma says I've done on that CV she wrote me. It was bloody embarrassing yesterday when Petula made me speak Arabic on the phone to that woman from the Dubai Embassy. All I did was clear my throat and slosh spit about my gob saying words that they used to have on the menu board down at Kebabish in Ilford. Eventually the woman just hung up. I don't know how much longer I can fool everyone here that I'm not really who I say. Every white lie you tell creates four more white lies. Uma Brunton-Fletcher makes it look so bloody easy.

FRIDAY FEBRUARY 12TH

***KITTEN'S TITBITS* HOT PARTY GOSSIP
FROM OUR VERY OWN IT GIRL**
Mwah mwah dahlinks! Oh yes indeedydoody this is Kitten here to tell you all about the proper amazing parties what I've been falling out of hammered this week. There have been stacks of them. One of them was after a movie premiere for the film *Body Impact*. It was a good movie and I liked it a lot and everyone said my new dress was well nice, it was a shiny dress and it was blue and

proper short and it cost £850 except it didn't really cost me anything 'cos I got it free 'cos I am Kitten. I can't remember any more facts about this week or nothing 'cos I was totally out of my nut for most of it but hey stay smittenkittens! Love you all like a mentalist – KM-J

MONDAY 15TH FEBRUARY

I thought I might get into trouble for Kitten's column. I tried my best to make it like Mariella would do it but it was proper hard to get it right. I think some little bits of it maybe gave it away. And when I came in this morning some people in the lift were laughing about it, but then at 10am we all heard that Britney Spears fell down the stairs at a nightclub in Los Angeles where it was 2am and all the paparazzi photos started coming through on the email and everyone in the office stopped what they were doing 'cos they needed to totally re-do the front page and take off the main story about the little boy who had been squashed by a bus on Oxford Street and replace it with a big photo of Britney with her ankles somewhere by her ears. That's the good thing about working at *London Alive* – it is proper busy and there's always someone who has made more of an arse of themselves than you.

I looked at Wesley's Bebo site today and there's all these photos of him at Digby his mate from work's, wedding. He's there with Sooz. Bloody Sooz. She isn't smiling in one single photo. And she's got a sensible dress on from Marks and Spencer like a thirty year old would wear or something and peach lipstick. And she's got her arm round my Wesley like she's the one bloody getting married! Well I hope Wesley remembers that although we had our ups and downs we always had a good laugh. And that wedding didn't look like much of a laugh in those AWFUL PHOTOS. I was gonna text that to him but I didn't thank god.

THURSDAY 18TH FEBRUARY

I spoke to Danny today. I said, ''Ere you haven't rang me for ages, are you blanking me?' And Danny said, 'Oh no sweetheart. I've just been a bit down lately. I've had this big argument with Christian. We're not speaking.' Well I thought that was well funny 'cos Danny is proper sensitive about his friends. He's not like Wesley is with Bezzie where they sometimes get narky with the other one and then eventually one snaps and punches the other one and then they just forget about it and go down the pub.

'Anyway,' says Danny, 'how's life at *London Alive*? I'm so proud of you Shiraz! Hey, I read Kitten's column that you mailed me about! That was bloody hilarious.'

I just groaned a bit when he said that. I didn't mean it to be that funny.

Anyway Danny says he's skint at the moment so he can't come out but once he's got paid in a few weeks me and him are going to go out clubbing! We're going on a date! Well there'll be a few of us. I'm going to arrange it for when Sean comes through to London. Sean loves clubbing too. Well I had to put the phone down then 'cos Petula asked me to ring Kitten Montague-Jones again and write her column. I reckon Petula was the only person in London who hadn't read my last attempt. So for the rest of the afternoon I rang Kitten seven times and every time she was being sick and the last time the only three useful words were 'Too much champagne'. And then she actually got quite rude with me. And I was proper angry. And the clock was ticking and they really needed the column to fill the page so I just thought I better keep it real and write it.

FRIDAY 19TH FEBRUARY

KITTEN'S TITBITS HOT PARTY GOSSIP
FROM OUR VERY OWN IT GIRL
Mwah mwah dahlinks! KM-J here to wiffle on about what I've been up to. Well I ain't gonna lie to you, I ain't done jack. I crawl out my pit about 5pm each day and my assistant makes me a coffee

and sometimes I'm proper spewing 'cos I drink too much bloody champagne and never eat 'cos I want to wear size zero hotpants that cost £650. Then Mariella rings to get my 'vibes and feelings' for this column and I usually tell her to piss off the first four times 'cos I'm blowing chunks down the loo. And sometimes Mariella gets the hump and makes the managing director of *London Alive* ring my mummy and then Mummy rings me and starts jarring my head big time and then I do it 'cos I don't want Mummy to take me off the inheritance again 'cos when Granny dies I'm in line to inherit most of Dorset. Anyway, what else can I say? It is proper brilliant being me and I bet you wish you were me too. Love you like a care-in-the-community case - keep it real, blud. KM-Jxx

MONDAY 22ND FEBRUARY

OK. OK. I never reckoned I was going to get away with that. But look, right, I bloody rang her like seven times and the last time she was well rude to me and said, 'Look Sharon, or whatever your name is, you're the writer, I'm the talent, bloody make something up, you little muppet!' So I did. And now the editor Georgina says she needs to see me in her office first thing tomorrow morning when she gets back from Paris because Kitten Montague-Jones has resigned from her column and she wants to know what we're going to do about that problem. Oh god. Me and my big gob.

TUESDAY 23RD FEBRUARY

I really wanted to skive off today and in fact never go back to *London Alive* ever again but Uma came in my room at 7am and started prodding me and said I should go down there and front it out 'cos it might not be so bad. And at least I should make sure I got all the money they owed me if I was going to get fired. Then Uma kept making Zeus come in the bedroom and wash my face with his big Winalot-flavoured tongue until I had to get up anyway. So I went down to *London Alive* and when I got there everyone looked at me like I was a dead hoodie, walking off to the executioner's chair or something. So I went into Georgina's office and she was on the phone apologising to someone and then I heard Kitten's name mentioned and realised she was apologizing about me and I felt really bad again.

Georgina put the phone down and looked at me. Then she sort of laughed. 'Shiraz Bailey Wood,' she says, 'take a seat. How are we doing today? Made any more It

Girls check into the Priory clinic with a nervous breakdown yet?'

'Yeah sorry about that Georgina, didn't mean it,' I said. It was like being in Mr Bumbleclot's office at Superchav Academy all over again.

'I think you did mean it, Shiraz,' Georgina said. 'I think you meant every word of it. It was totally from the heart, wasn't it?'

'Mmmmmsoz,' I said. And then Georgina burst out laughing and shook her head in disbelief. 'Shiraz, you have caused me no end of trouble! Kitten's father is good friends with the Managing Editor, y'know?!'

Well I tutted proper loud then 'cos I couldn't help it. 'I know! I know!' I said. 'But she never wrote the bloody column anyway. And even the made-up stuff by Mariella was a load of old crap. Just her going on about her bloody last bikini wax or new dress or something. None of it was real. Why can't you have someone keeping it real and talking about real stuff? What's wrong with being real?'

'Who are you?' said Georgina, peering at me suspiciously. 'Where did you come from? It says Mayflower Ladies Academy on your CV. I've looked it up, there's no such school.'

I went bright red then. This was a bad time to have done my speech about keeping it real. I'd forgotten about my CV. 'Oh it's got another name,' I said. 'People call it Mayflower Academy. It used to be called Marlowe Comprehensive. It's in Goodmayes.'

Well Georgina's eyes really lit up there. 'Marlowe Comp!? Marlowe . . . hang on, Superchav Academy?' she says. Well I must have nearly fell off my chair in shock. 'I've been there!' she says. 'When I was a rookie reporter. This kid with a ginger skinhead set light to one of the teacher's cars in the middle of the hockey pitch!'

'Clinton Brunton-Fletcher?' I said, nodding.

'That's him! Didn't he get the first ASBO in Goodmayes?'

'Yeah,' I said, 'cos I remember how proud the Brunton-Fletchers were about that. They had a buffet and everything.

'So what's happened to him now?' asked Georgina.

'He's in Chelmsford nick right now on remand for cocaine supplying.'

'Oh, excellent,' said Georgina, proper sarky like. 'That ASBO gave him a shock then.' And then we both laughed and she winked at me. I was starting to quite like her now. I reckoned she might be the only normal person in that office.

'So you're all about keeping it real then are you Shiraz?' Georgina says to me. Then she stops and thinks. 'Shiraz Bailey Wood: Keeping it Real. That's a good name for a column.' We both stared at each other for a moment. 'Go on Shiraz, keep it real then, and write me three hundred words by Thursday morning.'

MARCH

FRIDAY 5TH MARCH

KEEPING IT REAL WITH SHIRAZ BAILEY WOOD: SKINT

The dress I went out in last night didn't cost £650. It cost eight pounds. I got it from the sale rack in Ilford New Look. I got three quid knocked off 'cos the armpits smelled a bit like BO and were all stretched. I reckon some bird with proper wobbly bingo-wing arms bought it, left the tags, went dancing, then took it back after. And I didn't go to any flashy party last night either. I went to The Duck with my mate Uma 'cos you can get a double Oily Knob Whisky and lemonade and a minted lamb burger all for under four pounds.

I'm not a celebrity and I ain't rich. Get me? I'm just a normal person and I'm totally skint. Proper brassic park. I got £16.47 to last me till pay-day at the end of March. I don't even put the heating on in our flat if I'm by myself, I just cuddle our resident staffy Zeus 'cos it's cheaper. The other day I saw a homeless bloke eating a sandwich in a doorway and I felt well jealous 'cos at least he had a sandwich and I was having Primula squeezy cheese for my supper, squeezed on my fingers.

Anyway, I'm just saying this 'cos I think in London we forget how poor normal people really are. In London it's proper easy to get caught up in a world of thinking everyone can shop in Harrods and stand about in Veryveryvery VIP rooms pouring £350 over your heads like a wazzock.

But I've only lived here like seven months and I've seen some of the poorest folk in the world ever too. Like this bloke in an alleyway off Regent Street who sleeps in a pile of rubbish. And a cleaner at a big famous store who keeps her baby in a locker while she cleans loos. How bad is that?

So my advice is to not pay any attention to numnuts like Kitten Montague-Jones. They don't even pay for their clothes and parties and drinks anyway. THEY GET IT ALL FREE. So no wonder they look so bling. It would be good if for once in a while we made them INVISIBLE. Don't mind me or nothing. I'm only keeping it real.

shirazbaileywood@londonalive.co.uk

TUESDAY 9TH MARCH

***LONDON ALIVE* LETTERS!**

YOUR COMMENTS ABOUT OUR NEW COLUMNIST...
SHIRAZBAILEYWOOD? HA HA! BARE JOKES! WHO IS SHE? WHERE DID YOU GET HER — SB from PECKHAM.
LOVING DA COLUMN SHIRAZ — KEEP ON KEEPING IT REAL, SISTA! ER from WOOD GREEN
GOOD RIDDANCE KITTEN — SEEMS WE AIN'T THAT SMITTEN! DR from BRIXTON

WEDNESDAY 10TH MARCH

Oh my days, my column has really done AMAZING at *London Alive*! Georgina is well happy. She says I can stay till the end of my internship even though my CV is all total lies. Petula and Mariella are WELL HACKED OFF. And I got about two hundred and fifty fan emails too!

And right enough some of the were from total and utter fruitcakes and some were from blokes asking if I could mail them a picture of me standing about in the nuddy, but LOTS of them were from real people saying that they agreed with me one hundred per cent and they were skint too!

And Danny did something amazing today. He sent a bloody bunch of flowers to the *London Alive* offices with a card that said '*You are a superstar! From your biggest fan Danny Ps – see you tomorrow night for some serious dancing!*' And Sean arrives tomorrow too. It's is going to be the best night ever!

FRIDAY 12TH MARCH

7am – oh god. I can't believe last night happened. Sometimes I think my life is being filmed by a secret camera show. Sometimes when things get really really bad I feel like spinning around and shouting at passers-by, 'I know what's going on! You won't fool me! This is Punk'd isn't it! Turn the cameras off!' And then suddenly it dawns on me. This ain't no hidden camera show. This is real life.

KEEPING IT REAL WITH SHIRAZ BAILEY WOOD: BOYS

OH MY DAYS. OH GOD. Oh no no no. I have honestly given up on boys. It is official. I GIVE UP. I can't believe I have been such a collosal nimrod. I have been chasing this boy right for like seven months. Chasing him like a bloody bear would chase a man made of marmalade sandwiches I have. And I TOTALLY thought I was in there with him!

And OMG this boy had everything. He's well choong, clever, funny, excellent buns, good clothes and he likes all the same type of things as me. Well it bloody turns out now that he does like EVERYTHING the same as me. In fact he likes BOYS too. IN FACT, he's now going out with my friend Sean who he met on Thursday night on our date together!

And word of warning, if you are a girl planning on going out to meet the love of your life DO NOT, repeat NOT get tickets for a club called Quack Quack which is in Vauxhall on Thursday nights. Yes, indeed, it's full of men who look like models in tight T-shirts with great bums but believe me, they are NOT available to anyone with boobs or a ladygarden. It's like bloody being taken to the pick 'n' mix

counter at Vue Cinema and then told
you can't have no sweets you can just
look at them and drool 'cos you're a
diabetic.

My lovelife is a laughable SHAMBLES.
In the last twelve months my closest
thing to romance was snogging an elf
from the Outer Hebrides and his breath
smelled of garlic and we kept falling
over 'cos we kept getting the toes on
our curly slippers tangled up. After
that, I've had NOTHING. Not a sniff. I
am wandering in the sexual Gobi
Desert. And that would be OK but from
2am until 6am every bloody night I
have to hear my mate Carrie being
tickled by a reserve from Southend FC.

The worst thing is, I gave up a
proper amazing, loyal boyfriend who
loved me with all of his heart to come
to London. And sometimes I reckon I
made the wrong decision. 'Cos every
time I think of him with his new woman
I want to put my face inside the
Breville toastie machine and whack it
shut twenty times on my big stupid
bloody head. People of London,
I'm proper sorry to bother you with

all this. I'm only keeping it real.
shirazbaileywood@londonalive.co.uk

SUNDAY 14TH MARCH

From: dannychampionoftheworld1987@hotmail.com
To: theshiz@widebluevonder.co.uk
Time: 11.41am

Shiraz – it's Danny here. Mate I am so sorry. I have just read your last column on-line and I feel terrible. Shiraz you are the funniest, most beautiful, most inspiring woman I reckon I have ever met. In fact I reckon I fell in love with you like five minutes after you walked into Working Magic. If I was that way inclined I would snap you up in a second. But I'm not.

I'm so sorry Shiraz, I thought you knew. I thought it was just so cool how we never had to speak about it, like we just both had an understanding. Shiz, I hope you're not mad at me? Can we still be friends? My world would be a far more boring place without the legendary Shiraz Bailey Wood and I'm sorry to hit you with all this but I'm only keeping it real. With love – Dannyxxxxx

From: theshiz@widebluevonder.co.uk
To: dannychampionoftheworld1987@hotmail.co.uk
Time: 3.46pm
Of course we can, you daft git. Come over to my house

197

tonight if you're free. Me and Uma are watching *Legally Blonde 2*. Shizzlebizzlewoodxxx

Ps – if you're still with Sean, word of advice, don't get him talking about Kylie Minogue. I made that mistake in 6th Form and he talked for so bloody long that I woke up a week later covered in cobwebs and needing a haircut. LOL!!!!

TUESDAY 16TH MARCH

My mother rang me today for a chat. She don't normally ring me for a chat. We ain't that type of snugglywuggly mum and daughter, so I knew something must be wrong. 'Have you spoken to Cava-Sue lately?' Mum says to me.

'No,' I says. 'Why?'

'Well I wondered if she'd spoken to you about anything,' says Mum, ''cos she's sort of stopped speaking to everyone else.'

'How do you mean?' I says.

'Well she's just sort of stopped speaking,' says Mum. 'She ain't said a word for days.'

'Oh god,' I said. 'Something's gotta be wrong.'

'I know,' says my mum. 'I just can't work out what. She's got everything to be happy about too. Lovely little boy. Nice boyfriend. I can't understand why she's so bloody down.'

KEEPING IT REAL WITH SHIRAZ BAILEY WOOD: BABIES

I don't mean no offence or nothing but I think lots of us girls have babies without properly thinking what it's going to be like. 'Cos when babies are being all cute with little pudgy faces and big smiles then it's well easy to forget how much they change your life for ever.

And I reckon it must be well easy sometimes to forget that and just go ahead and get preggo. 'Cos maybe the boy you are with wants one. Or maybe you're just a bit lonely and you want something to cuddle. Or maybe you didn't think it would be so easy to get knocked up 'cos you thought all that boring crap the teachers used to go on about with sperm fertilising eggs won't happen to you. And then before you know it you're in the pudding club like my mate Kezia and then your life ain't your own life for ever.

The thing no one ever proper explains about babies is how

everything becomes like one big long never-ending army assault course. Like, say you want to go down Londis and get a Mars Bar?

Well, once it would have taken you seven minutes, but when you've got a baby, you've got to dress the baby, pack the pram, get the pram out of the house, get the pram up and down all the kerbs, try to get the pram into Londis which is too small to push a pram around, or leave the pram outside then hope the crackheads don't steal your baby, buy your Mars Bar, then set off all the way home again with a baby screaming its head off, needing changing and feeding and burping and putting back to bed again at the other end. It takes about an hour.

And sometimes the same boy who wanted the baby in the first place then changes his mind and says he wants to join the Navy and see the world. 'Cos that's what happened to my mate Kezia and her baby Latanoyatiqua. Now her babyfather Luther is seeing the world and Kezia is seeing the inside of bloody Happymums Community-centre Baby Café every second Tuesday if she is lucky.

I miss Kezia. She should have come to London with us lot and had a laugh. So I'm not saying like 'no one have babies' 'cos that would be stupid 'cos the human race would be extinct. But I'm just saying maybe give it a swerve when you're only young and push one out when you're like ancient and in your twenties instead. I'm sorry if I'm causing offence here but I'm only keeping it real.
shirazbaileywood@londonalive.co.uk

WEDNESDAY 24TH MARCH

I was coming in from work, walking up the stairs and I could hear Carrie on her mobile phone talking to someone. She was talking about Paramount Mansions and what it's like living here and she said that it was 'quite grotty' and she shared with 'these two girls she knew from school'. The way she said 'these two girls' really hurt me. It was like me and Uma were a pair of randoms she hardly even knew and that made me well sad 'cos Carrie has been like a sister to me for years and now we hardly speak at all. We just don't have nothing to say.

I just don't really understand what Carrie's doing with

her life. Or with Barclay. And the girls on her beauty course are the biggest bunch of wannabe WAG bloody brainless bimbos ever. All they're into is dressing up and trying to get their picture taken in nightclubs. The more Carrie gets like them, the less she is like me.

'Oh Ibiza, I'm thinking,' Carrie was saying now. 'I fancy a break after the exams next month. I've always wanted to go. It looks amazing doesn't it!? Yeah I'm looking at brochures now. Have a think, yeah? It would be great to get some girls together and go.'

I felt sick when she said that. She's never mentioned Ibiza to me!

Anyway, then Carrie says, 'OK Gazella, I gotta go, I'm going out to a party in Bloomsbury. But anyway, what we were talking about to begin with, yeah, I'm saying yeah, count me in for that apartment you're looking for. I never said to this lot that anything was for ever.'

So I walked upstairs and we looked at each other. And Carrie sort of cringed, but then looked like she was totally fine again. Then I walked straight into my room and closed the door and got into bed and wrapped my arms round my legs and lay there for ages. That's the thing with friends. They're not like your proper family are they? No one *does* say it has to be for ever. Well good riddance to her. Me and Uma will get a flat together. WHATEVER.

SUNDAY 28TH MARCH

Oh god. I had this terrible call from Murphy this morning. He sounded proper flustered. And that's not like Murphy. 'Oi Shizz, I know this is a stupid question, but is our Cava-Sue with you in London?' he says. I could hardly hear him for Fin screaming in the background. Screaming blue murder like he was proper starving.

'No, course she's not. Why would she be here?' 'Erm dunno,' shouts Murphy. 'It's just I just got up and Fin's in his crib and Lewis is at work and Mum and Dad have gone to Nan's and Cava-Sue has vanished and Fin is doing his nut.'

'No, she's not with me,' I said again. 'Have you rang Kezia?' I said. 'Cava-Sue sometimes goes down the baby café with her? Or what about Colette Brown? They've been hanging about a bit lately haven't they? Maybe she's gone there. Why would she leave Fin though?' Fin was really screaming now. Even higher and louder than before.

'Look Shiz, I ain't got their numbers, so can you ring them girls for me?' says Murphy. 'And I'm gonna try and change Fin 'cos he has done a big crap and he is well stinking.'

So I starts ringing around Goodmayes, looking for Cava-Sue. But no one had seen her. And every time I put the phone down my phone would ring and it would be

Lewis or Mum or Dad or Nan seeing if I had any news but I didn't. And we waited all day praying maybe she's just gone for a walk but then it started getting dark and I didn't know whether to go home to Goodmayes or stay in London and see if she showed up here. Well either way she hasn't.

And eventually at 11pm tonight we rang the police and told them that Cava-Sue was missing, but they didn't seem that bothered. They think she might come back 'cos most grown adults do. Well in the end I lost my rag and shouted at them. And now I'm sitting in my bedroom and Uma's making more tea and I reckon this might be the longest night ever.

APRIL

THURSDAY 15TH APRIL

The day that whole thing happened with Cava-Sue seemed like the longest day in the world ever. It was two weeks ago now. When I look back now it feels like we were all running around mad all day like Vin Diesel in an action movie. But I suppose if I'm being realistic what we actually did was a lot of staring and saying nothing.

I mean, for the first four hours of daylight that day I just sat glued to the front window in Paramount Mansions, hurting my neck to look down Paramount Road. The one interesting thing Cava-Sue had said to Murphy over the few days before she went missing was that she needed to double check my address in London 'cos she reckoned she needed to post me a photo of Fin.

Well I reckoned this was a lie 'cos Cava-Sue hadn't posted me anything and, besides, she texts photos to me. In fact I've got a whole collection of photos of Fin that I'd saved on to my phone with Fin resembling everything from a mini violent hooligan to a devil goblin. In fact there had been one stage when Fin had one tiny tooth popping through his head when he looked just like a baby walrus. But anyway, he was still my nephew and despite his screaming I loved him. I wished I could say she had posted me a photo of him, but she hadn't. But at least this made me think that maybe she'd been planning to run away and see me.

Well I waited and waited in the flat window and Uma made so much tea that in the end we were both buzzing our heads off. And at about 10am suddenly there was a noise outside and I looked down and I saw a sight that actually just made my eyes leak tears all down my face without me wanting it to. I wiped my face and nose on my hoodie sleeve and ran down to answer the door.

'You all right, innit?' he says. Then he turned around and double-clicked the alarm on his banana-yellow Golf.

'Not really,' I said. And he could see I'd been crying so he gave me a ginormous hug and I could smell his Kouros aftershave behind his ears like usual and that made me cry again for some bloody stupid reason.

We went upstairs and I put the kettle on again. And Wesley Barrington Bains II sits down on the sofa and says, 'So, right, you reckon she's got your address here, innit? And she definitely ain't anywhere in Goodmayes, innit. And she's left her mobile phone behind in Goodmayes? And Murphy reckons she'd been talking a bit about London?'

'Yeah,' I says and then I sat down and blew my nose again.

'And hang on,' says Wesley, 'Lewis says that she'd been talking about that time she spent the summer here years back too, innit?'

'Yeah,' I says. 'And Murphy checked the history on his Internet browser and Cava-Sue had been looking at websites about museums and galleries in the West End and in Chelsea.'

'How many websites, innit?' asks Wesley.

'About a hundred,' I says. London felt so totally stupidly massive that morning. I was so glad that Wesley had come to help me because suddenly I didn't feel so overcome with pure panic.

Wesley sat there for a bit and drank his tea. And he was asking proper sensible questions really, like someone off *CSI* or something. 'Is Cava-Sue still in touch with that girl Pixie, innit?' says Wesley. 'Ain't she in London, innit?' Bloody hell, I'd forgotten about Pixie! 'And there was that drippy bird Luella who she used to do her Drama course with years back. Didn't she move to London too, innit?'

I ran and got Uma's laptop and some pieccs of paper and we started making a plan. I sent Pixie a Bebo message and I was well happy when she got back in touch and gave me a bit of news. Pixie said she'd not seen Cava-Sue since Pixie got back from Australia. However Pixie knew Luella too as they went to the same clubs in London and Pixie reckoned that Luella reckoned that Cava-Sue sometimes sent her text messages and photos of the baby. So I asked Pixie for Luella's email or phone number but Pixie said she's impossible to get hold of and the best thing to do is catch her in her flat of a morning.

Pixie said Luella lived in Kilburn, north west London. So I rang Mum and Dad and told them I was going out to search for Cava-Sue and then I spoke to Murphy and he said he was coming into London too and he was meeting Ritu as she had a few ideas. Lewis was going to stay with Fin. Lewis was in a right old state apparently. He'd bitten all of his nails off and he'd been being sick with nerves.

Me and Wesley got in his banana-yellow Golf and it smelled like Magic Tree air freshener and we put on an Usher CD for some reason and he gave me some chewing gum and adjusted his central mirror and it felt totally weird 'cos it felt like we were just off to Vue or something and me and him were still a couple but now everything was totally totally different.

We drove to Luella's in Kilburn and I held the *A-Z* map and I was directing Wesley and we found the road and I jumped out. Luella lived in this weird little flat in a basement with two other girls. It was 11am and she looked like she'd just woken up. I asked if she'd heard from or seen Cava-Sue and I almost fell to my knees with happiness when she said YES.

Luella said Cava-Sue had turned up last night and had slept on her couch. And I felt so happy when she said that, but then the next bit she said made me all worried again. 'She wasn't in very good shape headwise, I thought,' said Luella. 'She wasn't making much sense.'

'Did she mention that she missed Fin?' I asked.

Luella sort of looked awkward and said, 'No, that was

the weird thing. She was saying she never had a baby. But I knew she had 'cos she texted me a photo when he was born. So I kept saying, "Come on Cava-Sue what have you done with him?" Joking like. But she just said she didn't have a baby and she didn't know what sort of drugs I must be on to imagine that.'

'Oh god,' I said.

'And then she slept on the sofa, but when I got up just now she'd gone. Apparently she said to my flatmate Lizzie that she was going to see some folk she worked with once in central London.'

I got back in the car and I was so knackered by this point I could hardly speak but I was sort of buzzing on all the worry and the tea and the new news I had heard. 'Well what did she used to do in London when she lived here?' asks Wesley.

'Performance art,' I says to him, shaking my head knowing how bloody unhelpful that was.

'What do you mean? Juggling and that sort of thing, innit?'

'Yeah,' I says. 'It was when she was doing that Drama course remember. She even went through a stage of standing on a box covered in tinfoil pretending to be a human statue.'

'OK,' says Wesley. 'Well that narrows it down a bit, innit. Basically we need to go anywhere where there is a big crowd what needs entertaining.' Then he started the car and we set off.

Me and Wesley searched what felt like the whole of bloody London. We went to Covent Garden and spoke to the buskers and street artists. We went to Trafalgar Square, Big Ben, St Paul's Cathedral and Buckingham Palace. I kept thinking I might see her walking along or even lying down somewhere being homeless in a pile of boxes but she wasn't anywhere at all. And I spoke to loads of different 'human statues' and performers and showed them a picture of Cava-Sue but no one had seen her today, even if a couple of performers totally remembered her from when she lived down in London and agreed she was 'a really lovely girl'. I felt like I'd walked miles and I was about to collapse.

In the end Wesley made us go and sit in a MacDonalds and he bought me my favourite meal without asking which is a Fillet-o-Fish meal and a milkshake then he forced me to eat it. And we sat in the window looking out on to Shaftesbury Avenue just staring at the thousands of people rushing by and I sat and watched as this creepy little guy was plastering up photos of nude woman in a nearby phone box with their phone numbers underneath for men to call and then I saw two blokes quite clearly doing a drugs deal right there in broad daylight like they didn't give a crap about the police. And I felt really scared again then for Cava-Sue 'cos London is a big horrible place if you've not got your wits about you. And as I was thinking all this and trying to slurp my strawberry milkshake my mobile phone started ringing and I looked at it and it was Ritu calling so I picks it up and Ritu says, 'Shiraz, it Ritu. I got her. I bwoody got her.'

We decided the best thing to do was maybe let me and our Murphy go and speak to Cava-Sue. Ritu said that she'd spotted her down on the Southbank by the River Thames, staring out into the river, looking like she was away with the fairies. Ritu didn't want to run up and scare her away. So she'd called Murphy who was searching the other side of the Thames bank and then she called me and said she'd keep an eye on Cava-Sue till I got there.

Well me and Murphy turned up at almost the same time. We met up with each other on Waterloo Bridge near the river and Murphy looked even taller and even more like a bloke not a boy than ever. He even gave me a little hug when he saw me and then we walked down the steps to see Cava-Sue together. And the sort of funny thing was when we both walked up to her I thought she might go a bit mental and try and do a runner but she never she just sat there and looked round calmly at us and said, 'Oh hello Murphy, hello Shiraz, I didn't realise you were coming to London today too.' So we sat down either side of her and I felt like laughing but it wasn't funny at all, it felt scary.

We all sat there for a bit in silence. And our Murphy reached out and grabbed Cava-Sue's hand and I grabbed the other one. We must have looked like a bloody prayer group or something. And I says, 'What are you doing Cava-Sue? What about Fin?'

And Cava-Sue just looks at me and says, 'Who?'

And I says, 'Fin, your baby!'

And Cava-Sue thinks for a while then she sighs a bit and says, 'Sometimes I think he's not my baby. Like there's been a mistake or something. He's not my baby. He hates me he does.'

'No he doesn't,' I says. 'He loves you, you're his mother.'

But Cava-Sue just shook her head. 'I reckon he's cried for about ten hours a day ever since I had him.' Well no one could argue with this 'cos it was pretty much true. 'I don't know what I'm doing any more,' Cava-Sue said. 'I don't know where my life's going. I don't know what the meaning of it all is.'

Well I really wished I knew the meaning of life to tell Cava-Sue but I didn't have it to hand at this point. But then our Murphy pipes up. 'I don't reckon anyone knows what they're doing. I reckon we're all just blagging our way through and hoping for the best.'

Now for Murphy this was quite a profound statement.

'Oh Murphy,' tutted Cava-Sue. 'You're only young! What have you got to worry about?'

So Murphy takes a deep breath and says, 'Well, if you want me to be honest, I am quite worried. 'Cos everything was going OK to be honest. And then I met Ritu and she has like proper changed everything. 'Cos I

214

can't stop thinking about her 'cos she is the most beautiful, brilliant girl ever. But she's from Osaka in Japan which is like six thousand miles away. And her student visa is up soon and she needs to go home and she has this sort of boyfriend in Osaka who her mum and dad love but she really doesn't. So I've been lying to Mother and skiving off school to be with Ritu in Kensington. 'Cos I love her. I love Ritu. And she loves me. But I think she's got no choice but to go back to Japan. And now I've got to stay here and get a job as a stacker/truck driver at Tilak's pakora factoy 'cos I'm well messing up my GCSEs 'cos I want to be with Ritu all the time. So I don't even think I can work in computers now like Tariq's brother did. But the stupid thing is that if I got a good job in computers, I could go and work in Japan and be with Ritu. It's one of them catch-22 thingies ain't it?'

Well me and Cava-Sue just stared at him. 'Holy crap,' said Cava-Sue. And then we all stared at the river. Then Cava-Sue looks at me funny and says, 'Why aren't you at work? Have you got the day off from the estate agents?'

So I looked at her and said, 'Well, seeing as we're all being honest . . . Y'know something Cava-Sue, I'm not an estate agent.'

'What?' said Cava-Sue. 'What do you mean? When did you stop doing that?' she says.

So I took a deep breath and I says, 'I never was an estate agent. That was a lie I told Mum. Basically, I came to London and I worked in Sunshine Sandwiches head office but then I got fired 'cos I was too gobby and I lost the company about two grand in vouchers. And then I worked on the London Eye but I was fired for "misconduct and compulsive lying". And then I was a golf sign holder for a bit and around that time I felt like killing myself. And then I worked as an elf in the House of Hardy grotto which sent me so doolally I started believing in Santa Claus. Which I still do now to be honest. And then I gave out free newspapers in Trafalgar Square and came home every night covered in bird crap and newsprint. And then I worked in a postroom and now somehow I am a columnist for a newspaper where I write about how crap my life is and everyone laughs at me and agrees. And I've spent all summer chasing this boy who has turned out to be as gay as the bloody hills and is now dating Sean Burton and they're planning a summer trip to Ibiza together. Oh and Wesley has found another girlfriend so I've made a gigantic pig's ARSE out of that too. And my friendship with Carrie don't exist any more. In fact I reckon she hates me. But aside from that, Cava-Sue, everything is FINE.'

And then we all sat there in silence for a bit. And then Cava-Sue started laughing. And then Murphy did too. And then I joined in. And then Murphy says, 'See I told you that no one really knows what they're doing. We're all just blagging it. I reckon the only thing all three of us have got for definite is each other. We're the Wood kids aren't we? That's one thing that's proper one hundred per cent definite.' Then we all sat and said nothing for a bit and I honestly felt like crying again and I thought bloody hell we don't let Murphy speak for fifteen years 'cos we reckon he's thick and then it turns out he's all wise like bloody Yoda off *Star Wars*.

Me and Murphy talked Cava-Sue into coming back to Paramount Mansions and having a bath and some sleep and some dinner. We all set off back and I texted Wesley to come and get us, and quickly rang Mum and told her the good news. Back at Paramount Mansions Cava-Sue fell asleep on the sofa with a duvet over her. And then it was 8pm and Wesley said he'd have to be going back to Goodmayes now. I felt sad that he was leaving and somehow I knew right away I was going to really miss him once he'd gone.

So I walked him to the door and said, 'Look, Wesley, thank you so much for today. You've always been so good to me. I'll owe you for this for ever.'

'Oh don't worry, innit,' he says to me. 'You know I'm always here for you.'

So I sort of groaned and said, 'No. No you can't be no more really, though, can you Wesley, this was just special circumstances. You go out with Sooz now don't you?'

And Wesley sort of nodded slowly and said, 'Yeah, suppose.'

Then we stood by the door and said nothing for ages. And then I put my arms round his waist and then I sniffed his neck and then I kissed him. Properly on the mouth. And he kissed me back too. And we stood there and snogged each other for ages.

'Why do I still love you, innit?' he said to me, when we were standing in the dark by the front door.

'I dunno,' I said. 'I still love you too.' And the thing was I didn't mean just as a friend, I meant that I loved him proper.

'So what are we going to do now?' he says. 'I dunno.' I said. 'Why don't you come back with me to Goodmayes?' he says. 'I can't right now!' I says, 'I need to work out what I want!'

But Wesley just rolls his eyes at me. 'You never know what you want Shiraz!' he groans.

So I says to him, 'Well you don't know what you want either, Wesley! Why are you going out with bloody Sooz?!'

So he looks at me straight in the eye and says, ''Cos Sooz DOES know what she wants don't she? She bloody wants me, innit? She says she wants me for ever! She don't want to leave Goodmayes or split up then get back together and do my head right in innit!'

I stood there then feeling proper confused and guilty.

'You need to work out what you want, Shiraz, innit,' said Wesley, but he said it softly not angrily. And then he kissed me on the forehead and I kissed him on the lips again and then he went home. And I started trying to work out then what I really wanted, but I never worked it out that night and I'm still thinking about it now, two weeks later.

MAY

TUESDAY 4TH MAY

Cava-Sue is feeling much better. That's proper good news! I was really worried about her. I mean I'm not a doctor or anything but I don't think walking about looking like one of those zombies off *Dawn of the Dead* mumbling 'Baby? I don't have a baby' is a sign of anything positive.

Dr Gupta says Cava-Sue is a bit down and that is perfectly normal after having a baby and he has given her something to help her feel a bit better. Dr Gupta says now he's had a proper look at Fin he reckons he's got something called 'reflux' which means he's got sort of mega-heartburn, so that's probably why he's been screaming and vomiting so often. Anyway, now Cava-Sue is happier and Fin is being less of a devil kid and he's even smiling loads now and making happy gurgly sounds some of the day and sleeping for five hours at a time at night.

Cava-Sue is so jacked off that Dr Gupta didn't notice the bloody reflux thing sooner that she says she's gonna wait outside the surgery and chuck a bunch of dirty nappies at his stupid Renault Clio. And of course she doesn't mean it, but I thought that was quite funny 'cos at least it means she's got her old fighting head back on.

Cava-Sue has told Lewis that him going to work and her being at home isn't working and that she wants to share the childcare 'cos she is going to have a career too. Cava-Sue is going to save the planet again.

She is applying for a job at Goodmayes Recycling Initiative as an enforcement officer where she's going to spend fourteen hours a week bullying people about their recycling boxes. I reckon she'll be good at that. I was only home this week for twenty-four hours and she was such a total pain in the arse guilt-tripping me out about drowning polar bears all the time that I wished she'd go missing again. I don't mean that of course. I'm joking. Honest.

FRIDAY 7TH MAY

Oh god, Mr Thicky-thick-thick Barclay has dumped Carrie. Well he hasn't even dumped her. He's been bloody CHEATING on her and Carrie's found out. She's found out 'cos it was in *London Alive*! Turns out that for the last two weeks Barclay has been getting off with Kitten Montague-Jones. And 'in an exclusive interview with *London Alive* today Kitten said that she 'hadn't intended to hurt Barclay's girlfriend' but she did admit that there had been a "bit of an overlap" in the affairs ending and starting.'

Poor Carrie. I tried to ring her but she didn't pick up. And she got a bloody C minus in her end of term exams too. I don't know why I feel sorry for her but I do. She's my bloody friend at the end of the day ain't she? The silly cow. It's difficult to be annoyed with someone when you keep finding Zeus cuddled up with their hair weave, thinking it's a some sort of chew toy. I hope Carrie's going to be all right. I'm gonna see if she wants to come to The Duck tomorrow. It ain't very glam or anything but I reckon she might fancy a beer.

MONDAY 10TH MAY

Ritu has gone back to Osaka. Murphy took her to Gatwick this afternoon and then he came round by my house in Whitechapel and sat on the sofa and cried like a baby. He's proper tall now, so I sat down beside him and tried to put my arm round him but it was like an elf trying to comfort a giant. 'This ain't over,' Murphy says to me. 'How can it be over when we both feel like this? Why does she have to bloody live in Japan? Why does the only girl I like live in bloody Japan!?' he says.

I told him I didn't know, but I reckon everything happens for a reason. In the end Murphy stood up and wiped his eyes and looked sort of focussed and said, 'Right, I'm going back to Mayflower tomorrow. And I'm going to finish my GCSEs. And I'm gonna study computers and then I'm going to get a job in Osaka and I'm gonna learn to speak Japanese and I'm gonna marry Ritu. That's the plan!'

'OK,' I said, nodding. At least he wasn't crying any more.

'And that all starts tomorrow. Don't tell Mother, whatever,' he says, pulling his baseball cap down and his boxer shorts up at the back so you could see the washing label hanging out of his low-slung jeans.

And then he left my flat saying he was going back to Goodmayes. I'm wondering if he went straight there or went via the arcade on the corner of Whitechapel High Street 'cos he never can resist an arcade can our Murphy. Some things never change with little brothers.

FRIDAY MAY 14TH

Today was my last day at *London Alive*. I couldn't stay any longer because there weren't any actual jobs going and this girl called Jocasta whose dad is a Labour cabinet minister has been pencilled in the diary for ages to take over my internship. Apparently she's an 'absolute sweetheart', so says Mariella.

Georgina the editor called me into the office at 5pm today and made me sit down and chat to her. Georgina said she's loved my columns and they've made her laugh out loud every time and that I'm really funny. Georgina says that I should keep on writing but I should get a proper journalistic qualification. Georgina says I should think about doing one of the journalism diplomas at one of the universities and that she would help me to apply if

I wanted and give me a reference. Blimey! I need to think about that don't I?

The editor of a national newspaper says she will help me get into college! That's not the sort of thing that happens every day to someone from Superchav Academy, is it? She gave me her business card and her email address and told me that her door is always open for advice. I've Pritt-Sticked the card in this diary for safe keeping.

MONDAY 17TH MAY

Clinton Brunton-Fletcher got five years in prison today. So off he went back to Chelmsford Prison and his solicitor says he'll probably do three and a half years if he's well behaved. So that probably means more like seven years then 'cos Clinton could cause trouble in an empty cell, let alone a cell with three other Clintons in it. I went to the court with Uma and we sat in the spectators' section and watched him go down to the cells. Uma just shook her head slowly as he went and said, 'Stupid bloody idiot,' under her breath.

Then we sat on the court steps and she smoked an Embassy Red and told me about what Mr Deng had been saying to her at the casino. Mr Deng says that he wants to keep Uma on and start training her for possible management. He reckons that one day Uma could run her own casino. Uma looked proper stunned and proud when she told me that. Then she flicked her fag butt on to the pavement and we both went off to the pub and had a brandy and Coke. I keep thinking about Clinton in his cell, sitting waiting for five years to be over. I don't reckon that's much fun at all.

FRIDAY 21ST MAY

OK – I've finally worked out what direction I'm going to go in. I've just called Wesley and told him. He was pretty emotional about it all, but I sort of expected that. He knows I love him. And I know he loves me. And I know that he knows that I know he loves me. And honestly, we can go round in bloody circles like that all day on the phone and it don't make much any clearer.

I came in tonight to the flat and I found Carrie sitting in the dark watching telly cuddling Zeus. Carrie has been around the flat loads more since her and Barclay split up. And she's not hanging around that much with the Butterz girls either.

The moment Barclay dropped Carrie and started seeing Kitten, well half of Carrie's so-called friends started siding with Kitten. 'Cos at the end of the day no one really wants to fall out with Kitten 'cos Kitten's like an It Girl who knows everyone, and Carrie, well who the hell is Carrie? She's just a total nobody from Goodmayes in Essex.

Well, that's what they all reckon. I don't think that. I think Carrie is still pretty special. She's an idiot sometimes but she's still pretty special.

'I got my Butterz end of term results,' she says.

'Yeah I know,' I says. 'C minus, yeah?'

'Yeah,' she says. I wasn't sure whether that was good or bad really.

'What does Barney say about that?' I said.

'Oh he's quite pleased really. 'Cos it means I can work as a qualified beautician in some places. Or I can go back and re-sit later next year for five hundred and fifty pounds.'

'Great,' I says, trying to sound optimistic.

'I'm sorry, Shiraz,' Carrie says to me all of a sudden. 'I've been a crap friend. I got right up my own bum didn't I?'

'Yep,' I said. 'You did.'

'I dunno why you never punched my lights out,' Carrie said.

'I wanted to, but you were never in,' I said. Then we both started laughing like clowns.

'London proper changes people doesn't it,' Carrie says. 'We were best friends before we came to London. Weren't we? Best friends since back in the day.'

'Yeah, 'course we were,' I said.

So then Carrie sits for a bit and says nothing and then in true Carrie Draper fashion hits me with one of her life-changing blows.

'Do you want to go to Ibiza?' she says.

'What?' I says.

'Ibiza. It's one of the Balearic islands. It's wall-to-wall nightclubs and fit men and beaches and parties. Have you heard of it?'

'Course I've bloody heard of it,' I said.

''Cos I just spoke to Barney about my exam result and he says I should go and get a holiday and then re-take the exams. So I goes, OK, Ibiza and he said, yeah, OK, no problem but then he said he'd rather you came too as you're the sensible one. He says he'll cover the flights and that as long as we go Easyjet.'

I sat and looked at her with my gob open.

'I can't go to Ibiza!' I says. But I really really wanted to go already.

'Why not?' says Carrie.

'I dunno,' I says. 'It's all just a bit sudden.'

'It's only for a fortnight. Oh come on. What could go bloody wrong with a little holiday in Ibiza. Hey, aren't Danny and Sean planning to go out there too? Ooh! We should ask Uma! And what about Kezia? I bet her mum would look after Latanoyatiqua. Imagine that? It would be so amazing. We'd all be in Ibiza together! Oh my days, I'm getting overexcited already!'

That's the thing that's not changed about Carrie. She has been leading me into situations since Year Seven of Mayflower Academy. But mostly good situations I suppose 'cos Carrie makes me do things that I'd never usually dare.

So we rang Uma at work and she sounded into the

Ibiza idea and said she'd ask Mr Deng for some time off. And Uma said she'd ring some of the Goodmayes girls and start looking on the Internet.

And then I remembered about Wesley Barrington Bains II. So I called him to let him know. That was the difficult part. Wesley says I can't bloody expect him to sit about Goodmayes all his bloody life waiting for me to get everything out of my system and still be there waiting at the end of it, innit.

So I said, 'Oh don't be tight Wesley, I've never been on holiday on my own just with the girls ever. Why are you being so negative? Less of the attitude!'

And Wesley didn't say much then. Then he said 'Oh Shiraz, well do what you bloody like 'cos I'll probably have forgotten about you by the time you get home, innit.'

So I said, 'Fair enough, Wesley. Well that's just a risk I'll have to take,' and then I put the phone down on him. And then me and Carrie got back on the Internet.

The whole gang of us are flying from Heathrow to Ibiza at 2.15pm on Tuesday June the 7th!

It's going to be WELL amazing.

Can't get enough of Shiraz?
Then look out for the first of her slammin' diaries

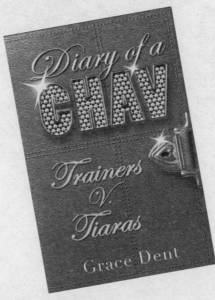

Diary of a
CHAV

Trainers
V.
Tiaras

Grace Dent

...TUESDAY – 8PM

Soapstars on Skates is on TV and our Staffy's snout is jammed up my armpit. Dad's got out the karaoke machine, Mum's setting fire to the kitchen – least that's what it smells like – and Nan has dropped off on the couch. Yeah, BORED!

But hey, Nan's got me a buff leather diary for Christmas! So now, I – Shiraz Bailey Wood – can write down all my 'goings on': hanging roundBurger King Car Park in Bezzie's Vauxhall Nova. Falling out with my hippy sister. Trying not to murder my little bruv. Definitely NOT thinking about school...
Keeping it real...

http://shirazbaileywood.bebo.com

Can't get enough of Shiraz?
Then look out for the second of her slammin' diaries

OH MY DAYS!

I've only gone and passed SEVEN GCSEs! Dad and Cava-Sue are chuffed to bits. Murphy reckons I cheated. Mum is pulling her best dog's bum face. She's not happy, I can tell ...

So, Mayflower Sixth Form here I come! Time to ditch the gold hoops and the spray tan and get myself a long scarf, some A4 folders and a new pencil case. Shiraz Bailey Wood is entering a new phase. Clever, sophisticated and definitely not skiving off ... Staying real ...

http://shirazbaileywood.bebo.com

OMG! You've gotta go and check out....

www.shirazbaileywood.co.uk

- ⭐ Read all about what's going on in Shiraz's world in her SLAMMIN' weekly blog

- ⭐ Join up to the TOTALLY MENTAL forum to meet and chat with other Shiraz fans

- ⭐ Exclusive BLINGIN' members' area for VIPs like yourself

- ⭐ Have your say and vote on what's hot and what's not, word of the week and much more... OH MY DAYZ!

Log on today at www.shirazbaileywood.co.uk
You'll be lovin' it – guaranteed!